MAR 0 3 2005

Call Me María

Call Me María

a novel

Judith Ortiz Cofer

Orchard Books · New York
An Imprint of Scholastic Inc.

Library of Congress Cataloging-in-Publication Data is available.

0-439-38577-6

10 9 8 7 6 5 4 3 2 1   04 05 06 07 08

Printed in the U.S.A.   23

Reinforced Binding for Library Use

First edition, October 2004

Designed by Elizabeth Parisi

For Mr. C.

Acknowledgments

This book could not have been written the way it was without the vision and support of my very cool editor, Amy Griffin. The task of being my second pair of eyes fell to my *apreciada asistente* Billie Bennet, to whom I am very grateful for her devoted attention to the writing. Special thanks go to John Cofer, who gave me his insights on the dynamics of a high school classroom, as well as technical advice on the subjects of math and science. His unwavering belief in the power of a good teacher to shape the lives of young people is at the heart of this book.

Contents

La Poesía

Y fue a esa edad . . . llegó la poesía
a buscarme. No sé, no sé de dónde
salió, de invierno o río.

— Pablo Neruda

Poetry

And it was at that age . . . poetry showed up,
and it was looking for me. I do not know, I do not know
where it came from, if it came from winter or the river.

— Pablo Neruda

Call Me María

It is a warm day, and even in this *barrio*
the autumn sun feels like a kiss, *un besito,*
on my head. Today I feel
like an iguana seeking a warm rock
in the sun. I am sitting
on the top step of the cement stairwell
leading into our basement apartment
in a city just waking
from a deep and dark winter sleep.
The sun has warmed the concrete,
rays falling on me like a warm shower.
It is a beautiful day
even in this barrio, and today
I am almost not unhappy.
I am a different María,
no longer the María Alegre
who was born on a tropical island,

and who lived with two parents
in a house near the sea
until a few months ago,
nor like the María Triste, the lonely
barrio girl of my new American life.
I am fifteen years old.
Call me María.

Sometimes,
when I feel like a bird
soaring above all that is ugly or sad,
I am María Alegre.
Other times,
when I am like a small,
underground creature,
when I feel like I will never
see the sun again,
I am María Triste.
My mother used to call me
her *paloma*, her dove,
when I was *alegre*,
and her *ratoncita*,
her little mouse,
on the days when I was *triste*.
Today I am neither.
You can just call me María.

Like the First Flower

There is one window at sidewalk level
from where I can see people's legs up to their knees.
It is where I have my desk, even though
it is supposed to be the living room.
Since my mother has not joined us yet,
I am the decision maker when it comes to our home,
the furniture, the meals we eat, even the household budget.
I keep our place in twilight when Papi is away.
I like its cavelike atmosphere. I feel safe
from the crazy street. From my underground
home I will watch the world go by until
I am ready to surface, *una flor en la primavera*.
I know that spring will come someday even to this barrio.
When it does
I will break through the concrete and reach for the sun
like the first flower of spring.

Letter to Mami

Querida Mami,

I keep hoping to get a letter from you soon. I know you are busy with your new school year, but I am so lonely here.

I read all the time. My English is getting better every day. I make lists of words that I like and I play the tapes of English lessons that you made for me. All day I talk to the walls. "How are you today?" "I am fine, thank you. How are you?"

My new school looks like a prison. It has a wall around it and bars on the windows. I like some of my teachers. I have a few friends. I miss the ocean, the sun, Spanish in my ears all day.

I know you understand that I need to be here with Papi because he needs me more than you do and because of the promise he made us that I could live with him until I finish high school and am accepted to a good American university. I think he misses you, Mami. I know he does not write letters, but he always asks me what you say in your letters to me.

I miss you too, Mami. I wish I were looking for shells on the beach. It seems we could always find something beautiful the sea had washed up, like a little gift for us. There is very little beauty in this barrio. I feel like I am doing penance. Do you remember when I was preparing for my First Communion and you used to drill me in catechism? I learned then that sometimes you have to pay now for a reward later.

Do not forget me.

Con mucho cariño, tu hija,
María

Scenes from My Island Past

Part One:

The Beginning of María Alegre/María Triste

I am usually María Alegre.

I like to play tricks on Mami. We will talk in English in the morning and Spanish in the afternoon. She is a teacher of English and a storyteller. She can tell stories in both languages.

We live in a *cabaña*, a little cement cabin, one of many that are rented out to people who want to spend time on the beach. We get ours free because Papi is the manager. He gets up before the sun is out to run a giant rake pulled by a tractor over the sand. People always leave trash at night. Sometimes Mami and I get up with him and do a treasure hunt.

One day I run into the sunny kitchen. I am wearing my *mambo* costume, I have painted my face like a clown's, lots of red lipstick and thick blue eye shadow. I climb up on a chair; Mami's red Mexican skirt is dragging on the floor. I am six years old.

"Can we dance today, Mami?" She gulps down some of her milk, leaving a red lip-mark on the glass. Mami sighs, both amused and exasperated. Mami places the bowl of steaming oatmeal on the table in front of me and pours herself a cup of *café con leche*.

"I want some." I pretend to reach Mami's cup, but she is

faster. Some coffee spills on the yellow vinyl tablecloth anyway. Mami does not say anything.

She usually laughs at my tricks. But she has been very thoughtful and quiet these past few days since she got the telegram from Papi, who has been in New York visiting relatives. Tomorrow, she will take a bus to pick him up at the airport in San Juan. While they are in San Juan, they will visit Papi's doctor. Papi has been sick, and the doctor told him he needed to take time away from his job.

I am to stay with Mami's mother, Abuela, the three or four days that they will be away. They will bring home a new car, she has added. My grandmother said I was the happiest baby she had ever known and started calling me alegre, which means "happy" in Spanish. For a long time I thought it meant "crazy." Then Mami started calling me her María Alegre, and I knew what she meant. I like to make Mami smile and laugh. I want her and Papi to be happy. So I have to be María Alegre.

"Can we dance today, Mami?" Music makes Mami alegre.

"Yes, María Alegre. After we have digested our breakfast I will dance with you." I know she does not feel like dancing. I have seen her sad look when she gets off the telephone with Papi.

"Can we play a Celia Cruz album?" I keep trying to cheer her up. She loves dancing to Celia Cruz's songs. She says that Celia Cruz is seriously alegre.

"Why don't you go play your Disney records, María Alegre?"

"I want to learn how to do the mambo today."

Mami and I clear the table. I tip the bowl of *avena* and lick the bottom. Oatmeal with lots of cinnamon is my favorite. I sprinkle some more cinnamon on my spoon and lick that too. Mami does not even seem to notice. Today, she does not think anything I do is funny. I help her wash the dishes. We hear a skip in the song that is playing, and I see the gooseflesh on my mother's arms. She smiles sadly at me. She loves those old songs.

I ask Mami to tell me more about Papi's *tristeza*.

"Hija, you have noticed changes in your father, no?" Mami speaks to me in English, saying the words slowly so that I can follow her. She knows that I will answer her in Spanish because even though I know English, I feel more comfortable speaking in Spanish. She and Papi talk to each other in very fast Spanish. But she thinks I should know English in case we all move to the United States. My father is always talking about moving to the city where he lived as a teenager before his parents moved back permanently to the Island. He has always felt out of step with the island Puerto Ricans, although he has been here so many years and married an island girl, an island girl who wants to stay on the Island. They fell in love because she spoke English very well; it was her best subject in school.

"Your papi is sad." My father used to be the most alegre one in our family. But ever since Mami told him that she was going to teach full-time at the Catholic school, he has become very quiet. "Yes, hija. He is sad, very sad. The doctor calls it depression. It is a tristeza that is very serious."

"Will he get better?"

"I do not know, *niña*. Tomorrow I will go to the hospital with him. He will have tests done. Then I will meet his doctors and try to learn what I can do to help him."

"Shouldn't I go with you, Mami?"

"You forget, María," she pats my hand with her soapy hand, "you have to go to school."

"Will he get another job?" Papi had said to us that he did not want to sweep the beach anymore.

"Not right away."

"Will you keep your job?" Mami was an English teacher at my school.

"Yes, the children and the sisters depend on me." This made her smile a little. She really loved teaching, and all my friends loved her.

The tiny smile on my mother's lips encouraged me to try to make her laugh. I turned my alegre volume to max.

"Let's mambo, Mami!" I grab the set of *maracas* from the wall where we keep them hanging on a nail "in case of an emergency party," my father liked to say. Mami finally laughs.

"My María Alegre is without a doubt a *loca,*" she says, hugging me tight.

Scenes from My Island Past

Part Two:

A Memory of María Alegre

Mami sits on the floor in the middle of María Alegre's messy room. As long as she does not bring food in, María Alegre is allowed to turn her space into whatever she thinks of for the day. Under her bed there is a huge suitcase full of costumes. Mami never knows what María will become when she goes into her closet to dress up. Sometimes she is a ballerina, sometimes a clown, but she is always a dancer. María loves dancing and music. It is Mami's job to choose the music for dancing.

"Ready?" María Alegre yells from under the sheet she has thrown over her head while she changes into a new costume. Mami gets up and stands close to the bed. Sometimes María Alegre will jump off the bed. She does not always land on her feet.

"I am ready, María Alegre," Mami announces. A very fast mambo song blasts out of the speakers. María Alegre jumps into Mami's arms, almost knocking her down. Then they begin to do the mambo. The mambo is a fast dance and you have to be able to move your shoulders, hips, and feet at the same time. Mami closes her eyes and tosses back her long, curly black hair. She takes her skirt in her hand and turns so fast that it fans out and María Alegre can feel the breeze and smell her special vanilla and cinnamon perfume. María Alegre tries to imitate Mami's mambo style, but she gets tangled up in her long skirt and falls in a bundle to the floor, her toilet-paper breasts rolling out of her blouse. Mami picks her up laughing, and on her knees, she shows María Alegre how to swing, sway, shake her hips and shoulders, moving her feet only a tiny little bit. Mami is a great dancer — everyone says so. And whenever there is a party, people make a circle to watch her and Papi dance.

But it has been a long while since they have danced together. When he comes home from work these days, he does not want to go anywhere. They argue because he wants to live in the barrio, where he was born, again. She does not want to leave the job she loves. She keeps promising him that when María is older, they will go to America. She wants María to go to a good college. She teaches María perfect textbook English so that she will pass the exams. Mami corrects María's pronunciation of hard English words that have sounds you do not hear in Spanish, like the *th*. "*Thousand*, not *dousan*, María. Put the tip of your tongue under your teeth and blow out a little air." María goes around practicing her *th* sound, sounding like a leaky car tire: *th, th, th, thousand.*

Mami misses the parties and the dances she used to go to with Papi. But María Alegre keeps her in practice. In the last month or so, María Alegre has decided that one more thing she wants to be when she grows up is a professional dancer; although to be a teacher like Mami is also something she dreams about.

When the mambo ends, María Alegre yells out, "Now a *bolero!*" Mami puts on an old slow love ballad by Felipe Rodriguez and the sad violin music fills the room. The singer sounds like he is crying while singing this song about two people who love each other saying *adiós, adiós*. Mami and María Alegre hug-dance to it with María Alegre laying her head on Mami's middle and holding her tight. Mami is short, only a foot and a half taller than María Alegre, who is tiny, so she puts her cheek down on María Alegre's head. Finally when the song is over and Mami tells her that it is time for her to help clean their *casita*, María Alegre does not protest too much.

"So that Papi will see it nice when he comes home?"

"Yes, niña." Mami has explained it all to María Alegre several times already, but she likes to hear things three or four times. It is not that she is slow — she just likes to memorize things. She can repeat almost anything you have ever said to her — word for word. It can get very annoying sometimes. "Papi is coming home to stay, María Alegre. But I have to go pick him up tomorrow. I will be away three days. Your abuela will be here in the morning. You must be nice to her, and do your homework without being told."

"Then you and Papi will come home in a new car."

"*Sí,* María Alegre," Mami says in a more businesslike voice. "*Pero*, now it is time to work."

Scenes from My Island Past

Part Three:
Flowering

The day came when I was no longer a child. By then I knew that la tristeza, Papi's sadness, had become a part of our family. He only sang sad songs and never danced with Mami or me.

"He needs to go home," Mami told me.

"He is home," I argued.

But she was right. His feet wanted to walk on the concrete of the city where he had been born. He complained of the sand that burned his feet all day long on the beach that he cleaned for strangers. He said the sand was in his clothes, his eyes, his ears. The sand made his eyes water and tears run down his cheeks.

"Give me snow any day of the week," he liked to say.

And Mami did. She gave him snow for Christmas of the year I turned fourteen. "Tickets to Kennedy, good any day of the week," she said to him.

He carried the white envelope in his shirt pocket for weeks, like a small white flag of surrender. I knew he wanted us to go with him.

"I will not leave the Island," my mother said.

"I cannot stay," my father said.

María Triste had to decide between parents, languages, climates, futures.

"Hija, what do you want to do? Will you go to the mainland barrio or stay on the Island?" they each asked me.

I saw my mother growing stronger as she planted herself more and more firmly in her native soil, opening up like a hibiscus flower, feeding on sand and sun. I saw my father struggling against the imaginary sand that cut his skin, I heard him losing his voice — *sand in his throat, sand in his lungs,* he said.

"I will go with Papi. I will explore a new world, conquer English, become strong, grow through the concrete like a flower that has taken root under the sidewalk. I will grow strong, with or without the sun."

Where I Am Now:
The Tides, the Treasure, and the Trash

El Súper and his daughter, we are famous to the tenants
whose floods in the bathroom, whose disasters always happen
at midnight, whose heaters stop working
on the coldest night.
On the coldest night, at midnight.
Papi is their hero with a toolbox. *El Súper*. And I am
his secretary, his hostess, always on duty before school,
after school, when the telephone rings at midnight
on the coldest night. *Linda,* they call me, Pretty Girl,
to get my attention, to get on Papi's busy schedule.
But I do not answer unless they call me María.
Please call me María, I tell them.
The truth is that all of us in this barrio are what the tide
brought to the American shore — from my father
who answers their calls for help late at night,
early in the morning, in winter, spring,
fall, and summer, carrying his heavy black toolbox,
and believes he is in his America,
to the homeless man who warms his backside
at the front door to the building. We are like seaweed
in the rising and falling tides
that is life in this barrio. The tides
that bring more and more from the other side

of the ocean, like the mixed treasure and trash
of bottle tops and rare seashells and smooth pieces of glass,
and things that poison and cut you, that Mami and I
would dig through with sticks on the beaches of San Juan.

Here Comes Barrioman

My father's way of dealing with my mother telling him that she may not ever leave *La Isla* has been to plunge into his new life here, although it turned out to be very little like the futuristic vision he once had of his *familia* in a shining home replete with laborsaving devices and technology making our lives easier; in fact, here we have traded down from the life we had on the Island — not much money because my mother is a teacher and that made us middle-class to what they call blue-collar life here.

And it is true that my father is all *azul* in his super's uniform. But he does not seem to remember his promises of a high-tech, steel-shiny future, and I do not remind him. I know that he is trying to find a way to keep his promise of a college education for me on the mainland. The price I paid was to live away from my mother and from the Isla we both love.

Week by week Papi is becoming more a part of this building, this street, this life. He is connecting to the people in ways that do not include me. He seems to be shedding his Island like an old skin and becoming Barrioman in blue, the superhero to the tenants, able to fix any of our decrepit old building's problems: leaky pipes, broken windows, broken hearts.

Spanglish for You and Maybe for Me

My new best friend, Whoopee Dominguez, speaks in the barrio way because she grew up here. I am beginning to hear this as a new dialect invented by people who can dream in two languages. I used to think it was broken English, but it really does have its own rules of grammar: *Oye, vamos to the marqueta ahora,* or *La maestra has me entre un rock and a hard place.* I mean, you have to dive in feet first before it starts making sense.

Papi has picked it back up quick; he spoke it when he was a little boy, before he went back with his parents to the Island. I am trying to keep my textbook English (what my mother calls it) so I can get into college in two years. But Spanglish is like a song you cannot get out of your head. It has rhythm, it has a beat, you want to dance to it.

"Oye, girlfriend, you wanna ir al mall today, whadda ya say?" Whoopee Dominguez is sitting on the sidewalk, pressing her face to the window that looks down on my basement home. Her eyes are big and green and her bushy wild hair is done in dreadlocks. Whoopee's face is like the sun at my window, lighting up my basement home. "Okay, Whoopee, let's go to el mall."

Spanish Class, a Lesson in El Amor

La señorita Stuckey wears makeup and jewelry in colors that I have seen on parrots and flowers in tropical rain forests: chameleon-green eye shadow, bird-of-paradise red lipstick, and earrings made of coral and purple seashells. Sparkling in her dyed-black frizzy hair, she wears homemade barrettes of eye-of-god designs.

Tight over her big chest, she wears lumpy sweaters made by the descendants of Incas who live above the Andes, the wool carried down the treacherous peaks of Machu Picchu by llamas and yaks, whose own fur is used to make the lining of those boots on the big, traveling feet of la señorita Stuckey.

Her skirts are woven by Ecuadorians and her concha belt of leather, punctuated by multicolored *lentejuelas,* is the handicraft of Mexican stay-at-home mothers. Her bracelets that click and clack and warn us of her approach are of abalone shells from beaches where she has spent entire nights waiting for giant turtles to emerge from the sea, heavy with the next generation, whose precious eggs she will cover with sand and watch over during one of her working vacations.

La señorita Stuckey sits on her desk, looking like she should be the American Tourist on the cover of an old *National Geographic* magazine. She speaks Spanish with an accent that sounds like the United Nations of Below the Border, and she lists the countries she has visited for us; the obscure *pueblos* she has discovered, the palaces she has entered, the churches, the huts, the caves.

Yet she never tells us about the people. In her tales of adventure there are no people except guides and drivers of cars and buses. There are never any tales of friends she has made, or of boyfriends. And I ask myself in Spanish, *¿Está triste? ¿Está sola?* Does she walk in those tired boots made from the skin of an animal that can only be found in the darkest corner of the farthest mountain in the tip of the point of the southernmost hemisphere? Is she always alone? She is always alone here at school. She walks down the halls alone, staying close to the walls, as if she were afraid of being accidentally touched by one of us. She eats her lunch of mango or guava juice and *tamales* from the barrio *bodega* alone in her classroom. She freshens her bright smile before each class and tells us that she loves the Spanish language, in a passionate low voice, like that of an actress in a *telenovela* (she has confessed that she is addicted to Univision), that she will travel a thousand miles to hear it spoken. In two weeks, when school lets out, she is going to San Juan on a cruise ship.

I send her some words telepathically: *Señorita Stuckey, gracias, adiós, buen viaje,* may you find *el amor* when you visit the place where my parents once found el amor, and then, I think, also where they lost it.

Letter to Mami

Querida Mami,

In answer to your question, so far, I do not have many friends because I hurry home after school to cook for Papi and to answer his messages from the tenants and finally to do my homework until bedtime.

My goal is to get into college and move into an apartment above ground where I can see the sky through my windows instead of the legs of people on the sidewalk, although you can tell a lot about people by the shoes they wear. I play this game with my friend Whoopee, who wears combat boots; she changes the strings to match her clothes every day. The game is called Instant History. We try to guess what kind of person is going by just from their *zapatos,* by the way they walk, the sounds of their voices as they hurry down the street.

Mami, in your last postcard you said you had been taking trips around the Island with your students, teaching them the English words for everything. I am doing the same here, trying to learn the words of my little world. I know your *estudiantes* are learning green, blue, sun, mountains, music, friends; I am learning gray, snow, dark, cold, lonely, mall, clothes, music, friend. I miss you and our Isla. I am taking care of Papi. He needs me, although he does not admit it. I know you love your work teaching English at *la escuela elemental* and do not want to leave your students. I made the choice to come here

21

with him. I will not forget you. I am remembering your English lessons more and more every day.

My maestro in English class, Mr. Golden, said that I was good with words! *¡Estoy alegre!*

Te quiere,
Your María

Letter to María

Dear María,

Yes, let us continue to practice our English by writing letters to each other. I am writing you this letter in a place you would love. It was raining today and I decided to take shelter in the library of the *Instituto Cultural.* I begged some paper from a colleague of mine who volunteers at the museum to write to you. I can smell the pulp of the ancient trees that went into the making of all these books, hija. Imagine me in a thick forest of book-bearing trees and a profusion of exotic flowers with blossoms the color of this indigo ink. The rain is streaming down but the canopy of green protects me. I would like to make you a tree house in a library. Whenever you felt the hunger for a story or a poem, you could climb down and take your pick.

The storm is ending, I must leave this enchanted place. But it will always be there for us, hija. Come see me in the summer and I will take you to our favorite places: *la playa, los museos, las tiendas del Viejo San Juan.* My friend has offered to walk with me. He is a historian, a very intelligent man. You may remember him from school.

Hija, I am sorry that we are separated. I know you understand why I chose to stay. It took me so long to become a maestra, and my work means so much to me. I know you understand. I wish you had stayed with me. But I respect your choice to accompany your father. You know you can come home to me any time. You know that I can tell if you are ale-gre or triste from your letters.

You ask me if I am lonely. *Un poco* because I miss you.

I will write again soon. I promise to visit you in the spring, pull you away from your books, and take you *a bailar.*

Te quiere mucho,
Mami

P.S. Send me your poems!

The Papi-lindo, Fifth Floor

I've got the look, like the song says, *I've got the look.* There are
guys who are born to the part. It is your *destino,* and you know
it from the start. First, it's the way your mother looks at you.
She might start calling you *papi-lindo* or *mi chulito.* She will
say *¡Mira, qué lindo!* while she's dressing you for kindergarten
and tell you that you will break many *corazones* in your life.
Your father will take the time to part your naturally wavy hair
just as he does his. He will yell at the women for treating you
like a baby doll.

"*Es un macho,*" he will say. "Don't tell him he's pretty. Let
him get dirty. He is a *machito.*"

Even your sister will treat you differently than other girls
treat their brothers. When she is not angry with you, she will
ask you for advice about clothes. When she is angry, she will
accuse your parents of playing favorites. You know she envies
your eyelashes, how they curl naturally while she has to use
one of those pliers things that make hers look like check-
marks. She envies your skin — which is bronze in color —
like a shiny copper penny. You are thin. You can eat anything
and not gain weight. You never get pimples. When she wakes
up with a blemish on her nose or her chin or her jeans won't
zip up, she will call you papi-lindo in front of her friends, and
it will be spit in your face. You blow kisses in their direction.
It is your way.

Papi-lindo, you are *un sueño.* Not tall, but not short, you can look into a girl's eyes, and that's all that counts. But female jocks don't interest you. You like a feminine woman, a girl who likes skirts better than jeans, a girl who asks you what *you* like her to wear.

You never try out for sports teams. That's for ordinary guys who have nothing better to do. You don't work out. It's not about physical power, that's too easy. What you do doesn't have anything to do with muscles, it's a mind game. It's a God-given talent. Either you have it or you don't. And you do. You get what you want because you are who you are. If you ask a girl why she will do anything to get close to you, it's not your body she'll mention, or your car, or where you live, or where you'll take her on a date. She'll say that there is something mysterious about you. *It's the way he looks at me,* she'll tell other girls, *it's how he makes me feel when he says my name.*

You always put on your best Spanish accent when you take the white girls out; your best manners for the Latinas — open their doors and you open hearts, like your Mami says. When you look at a girl and sort of lower your eyelids like window shades, they know what you're saying. Your eyes speak all the languages in the world. Plus you can dance to anything: hip-hop, salsa, techno — you name it. The rhythm of the Caribbean, of Africa, of el barrio, the Bronx — it's in your blood, papi-lindo.

Sometimes you will be teased by other guys because you like shopping better than shooting hoops. They will call you names. You will ignore their taunts. You will keep your head. You have money in your pocket from the part-time job at the mall boutique that gives you discounts on jewelry and shoes and designer clothes. You will always wear a thick gold chain around your neck with a big cross and that *azabache* your mother bought from a witch-woman in the barrio when you were a baby — a little black hand making a fist that will keep away *el mal de ojo* caused by the envy of others. You know who you are. You don't need to answer to anyone.

You know that you will always be protected from harm by the women around you. Because you are a *tesoro:* soft when you need to be soft, but when the time is right, you ask for and get what you want — there can't be any doubt that you are *un hombre latino.*

And here is the secret: Everything you learned about girls you learned from watching them. And you, papi-lindo, you can be anything they want you to be.

More Than You Know ¿Sabes?

Because my mother is a teacher of English on the Island, I learned it growing up: *pollito,* chicken, *gallina,* hen, *lápiz,* pencil, *y pluma,* pen — the little song we sang every morning, and what she taught her classes she also taught me. I have a thick accent; it makes people in school think I am not good in English. But I know more words than many native English speakers because I need words to survive.

Every day I look up a word I will use to protect me. I know the meaning of words like *underestimate.* I know it means to not give someone their full value. I know *prejudice* means to prejudge. I know what *advantage* means. I know that it is the *prejudice* of some people that makes them *underestimate* me; they *prejudge* me because I do not look or sound like them.

I know words in two languages. I will not give up either one. It gives me an advantage to know more than you know. I am also taking Spanish Conversation with la señorita Stuckey. I will not forget my first language. And now I know my second language well enough so that I am not going to be lost in America.

The King of the Barrio

The huge boiler my father keeps running through the long cold American winter sits just beyond my bedroom wall in the dark recesses of the basement. It is a real presence in my nights, a sleeping dragon that keeps me company with its rattling noises and constant need of attention. I have gotten good at reading its dials and guessing what it might need.

My father has begun to speak only in the Spanglish he grew up with. He was born in this city of Island parents who wanted to go back to their native land. Papi says he never felt at home on the Island. He says the other kids made fun of the way he spoke Spanish. He tried to stay after he met and married my mother. But la tristeza only left him when he came back to the barrio.

"*Es* very sad, hija," he has said to me. "Your mother and I are both Puerto Ricans, but not the same kind. There is not just one way to be a Boricua."

And I say only to myself: What kind of Boricua will I be, Papi?

"*¿Qué haces?*" My father's favorite question to me, "Whatcha doin'?" No matter how obvious it is.

"I'm writing a letter, Papi."

"*Pues,* tell your mother that I'll write to her soon. *Estoy muy* busy. *Muchos problemas,* you know?"

"Yes, I know, Papi." My father rules a kingdom of seven

stories, each floor is a foreign land. His loyal subjects tell him their troubles each in a different language, and Papi answers them with the same old songs. *Ay, ay, ay, ay.* They always seem to understand him. He is the good King of the Barrio.

I do not bother to tell my father that I am not writing to Mami about him.

El Super-Hombre

At times, he seems to be angry with me, but I know it is not me he sees when he is yelling at me for little things. I know that he is afraid I will leave him too like he knows Mami will.

At night, he meets his *colegas* at the bodega, to play dominoes with the men, he claims, but I know there are women in his life too. He is practicing his guitar playing and singing, transforming himself from janitor to balladeer for the nostalgic little groups of refugees from paradise — who yearned for what my father and I left behind — the idealized Island life of their childhood dreams and grown-up fantasies: the little *casa* in the country or by the sea, palm trees, green mountains, and ocean breezes.

Papi does not compose new songs; he only sings the old ones, playing the sad notes until he brings tears to the ones who claim that *machos* never cry and to the women who are like Amazons in their daily battles to survive in this place that will always feel like a foreign country to them even though most of them were born here. But they have been taught in Spanish that they are Island people, and they believe this myth because it makes them feel special.

Papi's music is also a magnet for the women whose city-hardened faces soften and their winter-dry eyes glisten with tears as they listen to his deep sad voice recalling for them a world they never really knew, one that as *puertorriqueñas*, they believe they should long for although some of them have never been there. Papi grows less triste with time because he is home. Home is where you need to be no matter where you are taken, the place that calls to you. He is the *Super-Hombre*, the Barrioman.

Letter to María

Dear María,

I want to share a *cuento* with you about a greedy baker who wanted to charge the starving man for the smell of his fresh-baked goods, aromas which gave the poor man pleasure and hope. He took the beggar to court to make him pay for what he was taking from him. The judge, to everyone's amazement, agreed with the baker. "If a man enjoys the smells of your labor, good *panadero,* then he must pay you in kind." The judge gave the poor man some coins from his own pocket and called both men to the bench. "Now, my brother, I want you to put those coins in your pocket and jingle them so the baker can hear the sound of money and thus you will settle your debt to the baker."

I was reminded of this story when you wrote to me about the game you play called Instant History, where you try to invent people's lives as you watch their feet walk by the window of the basement apartment, or just from observing them at a distance. You seem to believe that you may be violating people's privacy by imagining their lives and enjoying your fantasies. No, María. The world is a feast for the senses. *¡A saborearlo!*

Abrazos y besos,
Mami

What My Father Likes to Eat:

arroz y habichuelas
arroz con gandules
arroz con pollo
arroz con salchichas
arroz blanco
arroz amarillo
bananas, green, boiled and salted
plátanos, maduros, sweet and soft or
verdes, fried into thick crunchy chips.
Mangos, breadfruit, *y aguacates*
flown in and delivered by FedEx
right to the bodega.
Sí, we have some bananas today,
my father sings
when the blue truck pulls up
to Cheo's. And we are
right there to watch
the brown arms
of one of Cheo's daughters
place the Island soul food
in the store window,
bringing us who shiver
in the chill northern morning,
the memory

of warm breezes,
of trees heavy with fruit,
of ourselves
as a perfectly happy tribe,
under perfect blue skies.

When the sighs
begin to roll
through the small gathering
of mango worshippers
outside the bodega,
it is time for my father
to strum his guitar,
and begin his repertoire
of national anthems
for the homesick,
time for me
to run into Cheo's
and choose the ripest plantains,
the plumpest mangoes, while Papi
leads the other customers
in a sad tribute
to our fertile little Isla.

He sings of a paradise
awash in neon colors

where the sun always shines
and flowers
bloom forever.

My father, the barrio pied piper
sings of an island
that exists
only in their dreams.

In my mind,
I too carry images
of tropical flowers
in bright colors,
azul, rojo, verde, amarillo —
but my flowers grew
in real soil, in a real place;
flowers that blossomed
and wilted, real flowers
that need the rain
as well as the sun
to live.

I have the colors
of my Island
tattooed inside the walls
of my head.

And that is one
of the ways that Island
and the mainland Puerto Ricans
are not exactly the same,
we carry different islas
inside us, yet it is
the same Island
that we love, and
we love it
in the same way.

Picture of Whoopee

Hair wild as hurricane winds over the Caribbean.
Skin, a bright new penny.
Eyes, black, ebony, three A.M. on a clear night black;
deepest part of the ocean black, almond-shaped
black mirror. "Look into my eyes, María," Whoopee talks me
out of my black moods and my dark days. "Follow me,
María." She pretends to be Whoopee the Magnificent,
Sorceress and Mistress of the Universe. I pretend I am
being propelled out of my sadness
like a sleepwalker, controlled by eyes
like two black laser beams. I follow Whoopee
into the sunlight
where she opens that *mouth,*
painted Puerto Rican red, and lets out
a glass-shattering Tarzan howl, or maybe
it is a sort of yodel from the Swiss Alps.

It is a song too,
a wordless scatting song half jazz, half salsa,
intended to wake me out of my apathy,
and everyone on the block out of our boring lives.
Sometimes her call is high pitched, other times
soft and mournful like a dove. Whoopee
is a one-woman band, mainly horns, trombones,
sometimes a flute. Other people whistle or hum,

Whoopee belts out musical notes. The sadder
Whoopee is, the angrier Whoopee is,
the louder she yodels. Whoopee
sometimes sings so long and so hard
that her voice sounds like a rusty hinge on a door.
She moves like a cat,
she is built low to the ground. She stalks
and pounces on life, takes steps two at a time.
I have seen Whoopee
leaping from rooftop to rooftop
in my dreams. I have seen her stop bullets
from a drive-by shooting with her bare hands,
Whoopee the Magnificent! I have seen her
stop the woman who just moved in our building, the one
with the wild look in her sunken eyes, from hitting
her little girl. Whoopee,
The Puerto Rican Superhero,
I have heard her send her powerful voice
up from the street and into the crying child's room.
I have heard her call out a warning
to the wild-eyed woman, "You will spew toads
and worms if you say ugly things to your child,
and you will turn into a warty frog yourself
if you hit your little daughter
ever again."

Whoopee, my best friend and my hero
fears nothing and no one. My friend Whoopee
fears nothing in the world except mirrors in her path.
She turns away from her own reflection. Whoopee
fears herself. She is afraid
that if she does not make us laugh
we will laugh at her.
She does not see her own beauty.
She performs for us. She gives us herself
as a clown. This is her gift and her secret
sadness. Whoopee does not know
her beauty. She thinks we will not love her
unless she is louder, faster, and stronger
than anyone else. Whoopee
does not know
her own beauty.

If Whoopee could go back in time
and walk by Frida Kahlo on a street
in Mexico, in a place where her brown skin,
wild black hair, and small solid body
were like those of goddesses and queens
sculpted into the sides of temples,
she would be immortalized in a painting called

Girl with the Black Pearl Eyes.
Niña de los ojos
como perlas negras.

Doña Segura, Costurera, Third Floor

Doña Segura is nearly blind, but she embroiders like an angel in patterns her fingers remember. For every birth, baptism, and wedding, she has a gift that cannot be bought at any store. She does it now because she wants to. For forty years, she worked in factories to support her five children and put them through school. She is almost blind from that work, collecting a small pension and sitting in a corner of her daughter's apartment working on her art by touch. When she calls out a color, *amarillo, azul, verde, rojo*, one of her granddaughters threads her needle.

I tried to buy a handkerchief from her, and she asked me what the occasion was. I said none and she would not sell it, but she did ask me when my birthday was and she did not forget. On that day, many months after we had talked about it, I found a package at my door. Doña Segura had gotten her daughter to address a box to me. *To: María Alegre, El Basement.* Her needlework is magical. On a pillowcase, she had embroidered an orange sun either setting or rising over a blue horizon or blue waves. I lay my head on Doña Segura's dream catcher every night. It reminds me of the Island women before Mami, before me. Doña Segura's threads connect me to my Island, the colors enter my sueños reminding me to dream in Spanish so I never forget where I came from. *Amarillo, azul, verde, rojo*, I say to myself as I fall asleep.

Bombay, San Juan, and Katmandu

Uma is from India and lives on the first floor above us. She and her mother, a widow, are learning to dance salsa from tapes. They both want Puerto Rican husbands, American men who look like Indians. I hear their feet above me, little bells and tiny cymbals keeping time, and a male voice above the music, "It's all in the hips, it's all in the hips." They are drunk on American freedom. Barefoot, dancing salsa steps with undulating Ganges-hips, daughter in red-and-gold sari, mother in widow white, they wear bells on their ankles, *it's all in the hips, all in the hips*. But Indian hips want to belly dance. I have seen how those Indian hips just want to make a circle when a mambo wants you to stop halfway and bring it back.

Some of the Latinas in our building complain about the pungent aromas of Indian spices that have permeated the plaster on the old walls in our building, weaving in and out of our apartments like saffron threads, rising through cracks and inside pipes, through vents and old bullet holes, so that even as we swallow our *arroz y habichuelas,* our *pollo frito,* and our *tostones,* all we are tasting is curry, curry, curry. *It is all in the spices,* the women say, *all in the spices.* It does not bother me. I dream to the aromas of India. I am taken by my nose and imagination to cities of hammered gold-and-blue many-armed goddesses by my nose: Nepal, where the beautiful god Vishnu-Narayana lives, Bombay, silk saris, palaquins, maharajahs and a trip to Katmandu — when you don't how far some place can be, you are going to end up in Katmandu. I also know about the three sacred rivers. There are the Ganges, the Jamuna, and the Saraswati — names like songs sung in a foreign tongue in the map I have looked up.

Uma trades Indian secrets about beauty, men, and sex, and gives me prints of gods and goddesses making love in exchange for American history lessons she comes to get like cups of sugar, facts she must collect for their citizenship test. She also brings me rudrashka beads and bangles, and tonight an iridescent cloth I can wear as a skirt or scarf, or even hang on the wall. Uma of the bronze skin, nose ring, turquoise sari, carries her U.S. Department of Immigration and Naturalization manual like a holy book in her hands.

Beautiful Uma knocks softly on my door at study time, when she knows I will have my schoolbooks in a circle around me on the floor, my father will be at his dominoes game at the bodega, and her mother will have her veil pulled over her head, kneeling in solitary meditation. Study-time Uma puts her long-fingered palms together, bows her head slightly in greeting. She has many questions for me: George Washington and Washington D.C., civil rights and the Civil War; the Constitution and the colors of the flag; and how do Puerto Ricans make rice appear orange? I tell her about the capital city, Martin Luther King, Jr., and the many uses of *achiote* in Puerto Rican cookery. Achiote wins as the theme for her lesson. We look it up and find out that the Indians of the Caribbean used the spice to decorate their bodies. This excites Uma who wants me to know that our cultures have something in common. She tells me about henna and we draw designs on our hands and feet with our black ink pens.

Do I look Latina? Uma wants to know. *Do I look Indian?* I ask her.

Golden English:
Lessons One and Two
and Two-and-a-Half

Lesson One:

"Everything I will say will be in declarative sentences," declares Mr. Golden.

There are more than one million words in the English language.

All the poems yet to be written are contained in the dictionary.

A poem is made by choosing the best words and putting them in the best order.

Words are weapons.

Words are tools.

Mr. Golden hands us a list. "Make declarative sentences from these words," Mr. Golden declares.

1. contains a universe
2. sand, concrete, horizon
3. I dream
4. blue, clear

My brain contains a universe.
I dream in Spanish of white sand beaches.

The ground I walk on is hard concrete,
but between the tall buildings, on a clear day,
I can still see the blue horizon.

"María, you are a poet," declares Mr. Golden.

Lesson Two:

Mr. Golden's eyes look tired today. He works as a singer in a band after school. He sang at assembly last week. His voice is like chocolate ice cream, like warm honey, like the golden light of the sun at the end of a winter's day.

"Class, these are imperative sentences," says Mr. Golden.

Sit up straight, Raquel.
I will have to see you after school, Miguel.
Do not use such language in my classroom, Michelle.
Speak up, María.
Look at me, Chanté.
I demand silence in this room!

Lesson Two-and-a-Half:

The Imperative Rap

Mr. Golden is out in the hall, reprimanding Rickie "the Papi-lindo" Moreno for manicuring his nails in class, and Whoopee decides it is time to entertain us. Taking Mr. G.'s place in front of the class, she raps to today's lesson:

Look here, this here
is an im-pe-ra-tive.
You there, I'm givin' you a sentence:
ten to twenty, no chance o' parole.
Look here, this here
is an imperative.

The class gets into it, chanting *this here is an imperative, no chance o' parole.* Whoopee is about to go into a second verse when we hear a deep voice joining in. It is Mr. Golden, grinning as he shuts the classroom door.

Go on, Ms. Dominguez. I'm going to ask you to take over the class for today. And he sits down at Whoopee's desk.

I believe you left off with *no chance o' parole.* Mr. Golden joins in the rapping, tapping out a beat on the desktop. *Look, here, this here . . .* Mr. Golden's deep voice is like a wave we are all riding. I see that almost everyone is moving with him (Papi-lindo is fuming in his back-row seat, pretending that he is interested only in his nails, which he is examining one by one). Even Uma joins the song, *no chance o' parole,* giggling at the silly words, winking at me as she points to Whoopee, who is now whirling as she sings, and soon Mr. Golden will have to say, Whoopee Dominguez, stop!

An American Dream

Uma, Whoopee, and I are walking to the bus stop. We will go to the mall today. Uma is wearing what looks like blue pajamas. She laughs when Whoopee tells her she likes her pj's. It is called a *salwar-kameez* — Uma explains — what Indian women wear when they want to be comfortable.

"The sari is a very complicated garment," Uma tells us.

Whoopee is in her most comfortable shopping clothes too — neon-green vinyl skirt, Puerto Rican–flag T-shirt, and her favorite red high-top sneakers.

"So why wear *complicated*?" Whoopee asks Uma. "Why, can'tcha?"

"My dear Whoopee," Uma explains patiently, "in India clothes are a statement about who you are. What you wear tells people where you are from, what dialect you speak, who your people are. . . ."

"Girlfriends, look at me." Whoopee steps in front of us, does her imitation of a model, twirling and showing us her front side and her backside. "What you think o' my statement? Can'tcha tell where I come from?" She points to the flag of Puerto Rico on her chest. "Where I'm coming from?"

"We know everything about you from your clothes, Whoopee," I tell her, taking her hand while Uma grabs the other hand (the bus is about to leave without us), "including what language you speak!"

"You call it Spanglish, María. I call it American. I speak American!" Whoopee is already making up some words to the rap song we will have to hear all day.

While we look at the stores in the mall, Uma tells us about her dream. In the dream, a boy with skin the color of copper had taken her to the roof of our building to show her the night sky. Instead of the usual constellations, the stars formed the map of America. She recognized New York, Chicago, and Los Angeles, California. The beautiful young man had said to Uma, Let us climb on your flying carpet and go for a ride.

"What happened next?" Whoopee wants to know, but Uma has fallen silent in front of a shop window where Ricky Moreno is dressing a dummy.

"That is the boy in my dream," Uma says in a strange low voice. I look at her as she watches the papi-lindo of our building struggling to fit a turtleneck sweater over the head of a tall male dummy. The dummy stares without eyeballs at us while Ricky practically decapitates him. It is almost impossible not to burst out laughing. But I look at Uma's eyes and they are big and filled with tears. Whoopee is shaking her head and looking at me. Big mistake! is what we are both thinking. Too late. Ricky has discovered his audience. He is now posing behind the glass for our amusement. He imitates the dummy's pose, standing perfectly still, staring with un-blinking long-lashed eyes at Uma, his copper skin shiny from perspiration that reflects the lights. Soon several other girls have stopped to look at the living doll in the window. It is the papi-lindo doing what the papi-lindo does best.

"It is the boy in my dream," Uma repeats, speaking to no one in particular.

"More like a nightmare," Whoopee says in a disgusted tone and pushes both Uma and me toward the movie theater. They are showing *American Beauty.* It costs only one dollar since everyone in the whole world has seen it except us.

The Power of the Papi-lindo

You've heard of the Latin Lover. Men with eyes like tractor beams, like the kind they use on the starship *Enterprise* to pull in stuff from outer space. This is what I said when Whoopee, Uma, and I were watching *Star Trek: TNG* and Uma kept breaking into tears because Ricky Moreno had promised to call her after he talked her into going up to the roof with him. That was a week ago, and he has not even looked at her at school.

Whoopee said, "Space debris. That's what they use tractor beams to pick up." That was too much for poor Uma, who ran upstairs to her apartment to cry her heart out by herself. "You really believe that stuff about Latin Lovers, girlfriend?" We heard some footsteps out on the sidewalk and saw a bunch of guy feet go by — among them, Ricky Moreno's shiny Italian designer shoes.

"Two hundred bucks, no less." Whoopee is a shoe collector herself, mostly thrift store finds, so she knows expensive footwear when she sees it, especially in front of her nose.

"I have heard that there are some Latino men who can make women do anything they want."

"Whaddaya mean, they use voodoo or something?" Whoopee's parents run the *botánica* in our barrio. It is a sort of magic store and drugstore combined. They sell everything from scented alcohol that is good for headaches and for driving away evil spirits to Vicks VapoRub and throat lozenges. Whoopee claims she does not believe in any of it although she has a collection of candles in her room with a spell for everything you can think of written on them: *para el dinero, para el amor, para hacer desaparecer sus enemigos. For decoration only,* she has told me.

"No, I think it is a talent they develop. They have to learn to be Latin Lovers, I think."

"What kind of talents?"

"How to look at a girl like she is the most beautiful woman in the world. How to say the right thing. I think it helps if they can sing and play the guitar."

"Like your father?"

"I don't think of my father that way. *Bueno,* he can be that way sometimes. I'm really talking about guys like Ricky Moreno. I think he is a Latin Lover apprentice. Look."

We both climbed on my desk and peeked up. There, sitting on somebody's car, were the papi-lindo and two of his friends. They were practicing a song in Spanish. But when they saw a girl coming (pink high heels, skirt so short we could not see the hem from the half-view we had of her), they would stop so the papi-lindo could go into his Romeo act.

"*Mamacita,* you are a work of art. *Mi amor,* slow down, *por favor.* Let me at least have a good look at what heaven must be like."

"Gross, that's sick. She ain't gonna fall for that crap," Whoopee hisses.

"Take a look."

We watch as Miss Pink Heels takes slower and slower steps. We hear Ricky tell his buddies to take a long walk. Then we see the two pink high heels and the two shiny black Italian shoes meet like two couples about to dance.

"Who is that?"

At first, I think Whoopee is asking who is the girl Ricky has snared with his Spanish love song he throws out like Spider-Man, wrapping her in a cocoon of amor, Mamacita, *ven, ven, ven*. But what Whoopee hears is the sound of someone sobbing. We both know it is Uma, who watches the street all the time for a glimpse of her love. She too has seen the action in front of our building. That is when I decide I need to have a talk with Ricky.

When I tell Whoopee, she says I should arm myself before I confront the powers of evil. I have to laugh at how dramatic she can get sometimes.

"Arm myself? How, Whoopee? Will you lend me your laser sword?"

"I'll be right back." She runs up the stairs with a look of fierceness on her face that reminds me of Xena, Warrior Princess.

I decide it is now or never. I will tell Ricky that he has to tell Uma that he does not love her and release her from his papi-lindo spell. Or else. Or else? By the time I climb the steps up to the street, my chest is beating like Ricky Ricardo banging on that drum on an old *I Love Lucy* rerun. I see him holding Miss Pink Heels against somebody's car. The girl has legs up to her earlobes. I recognize her as one of the cheerleaders at our school, Miss School Spirit. Everything she says has an exclamation point at the end. Ricky is rocking her in his arms and humming a tune I think I recognize. *America the Beautiful*? I heard that some vampire bats use ultrasonic waves to hypnotize and confuse their prey, and then they sink their fangs into their necks, no struggle.

"Hey, Ricardo!" I get his attention right away like I knew I would because only his parents use his full name; he is programmed to stand at attention when he hears it. The girl in the pink heels almost loses her balance when he pushes off the car hood where he's been lounging with her in his arms.

When he sees it's just me, he puts on an attitude again, but I've already seen his scared mama's-boy face.

"What? Whatcha yellin' out my name for, girl? It'd better be fire in the building, or is your old man needin' a little help with the pipes and the ladies today?"

"I need to talk to you. ALONE." I am using my best assertive voice. I have been taking lessons from Whoopee on how to make myself be heard. I run up the front steps and into the lobby before he can ask any more questions. I watch through the glass as he kisses the girl and sends her off, looking a little wobbly on her feet — she got off easy from her encounter with the papi-lindo — she could have ended up wrapped up in a sticky little love-cocoon, hanging over a bottomless pit by a silk thread.

I see him hike up his pants, then bend down to rub one of his shoes. The streetlight comes on suddenly as dark clouds cover the sky. He seems to be standing in a spotlight. His black hair reflects blue sparks like a mirror. He stands still for a few seconds as if he knows that he has an audience. Lightning splits the sky, beams of light from his fingertips as he combs back his hair. My scalp prickles; I feel hairs standing straight up on the back of my neck. I feel the floor tremble under me. Roll of thunder, sheets of rain, and quickly he is coming into the small entryway to our building, moving closer to me, too close.

"Ricardo. I just have one thing to say to you. Stop hurting Uma. Tell her you do not really love her . . . stop."

He corners me. I am against the wall, his arms above me, his silk shirt covering me like a red tent. I say stop at least three times before he presses his chest to my ear. I can smell the ocean now, I can taste the salt on my lips, I begin to hear music. You will think I am crazy when I tell you this — it was coming from inside his chest. I feel his mouth on my hair, his lips moving. I stand real still because I know that he is singing the words to a song I should know. I think it is my favorite Rubén Blades *canción, "Piensa en mí."* How did he know, how could he know what these words do to me? And where is that music coming from?

"María," I hear him say my name and it sounds far away as a dream, "María." I know that soon I will remember all the words to my favorite song and I will want to hear him sing it to me, so before he starts the second verse, right after the refrain, *piensa en mí, piensa en mí, piensa en mí,* I say, "You have to stop. . . ."

To my surprise, he does let go of me, but only because he has heard footsteps descending the stairs. It is blind Doña Segura being led down by her granddaughter, a thirteen-year-old who already wears red lipstick and streaks her hair purple. The old woman hesitates halfway.

"Qué cosa," she says. "I thought I smelled the ocean. It must be the rain. Is it still raining, Jessica?"

"Sí, Abuelita." Jessica looks at me, then at Ricky, and grins like the devil. "I thought I smelled a week in Jamaica myself." She winks at Ricky, who does his hike-up-pants-smooth-back-hair-sneer routine for her.

"Is that you, Ricardito?" Doña Segura walks slowly but seems to know exactly where he is standing. She puts a hand on his cheek. He brings her wrinkly palm to his lips and kisses it. "Ay, hijo," she says, "you remind me of every summer day I have known. And I have known many. *Dios te bendiga.*"

"Amen," answers Ricardo, in his best imitation of an altar boy.

By the time Doña Segura and Jessica have opened their giant red umbrella and left the building, I think that I have snapped out of my papi-lindo trance; but the papi-lindo disagrees, he thinks he can hypnotize me again. He turns on his tractor beams full power in my direction.

"Piensa en mí," he says, "imagine you and me in another place, María. A place where you have never been. *Ven, ven, ven, María."*

The way he says my name. *María, María, I just met a girl . . .* just like the song in *West Side Story,* it sounds like a song, like a prayer. Again, I start to feel like the law of gravity has been suspended. Then, suddenly, Whoopee's Tarzan yell makes us both jump. She is standing at the top of the landing. She does it again, only louder. It's either her glass-shattering voice or the thunder that makes the glass rattle. Whatever it is, I can see that Ricardo has had enough. He pretends he has not really jumped out of his skin. He pulls away from where he had me glued to the wall. He looks at me as he smooths back his wet hair and tucks his designer shirt into his designer pants. He leans down to wipe a drop of water off his designer shoes. He looks me over with a sarcastic smile as he turns to go.

Finally, he looks disapprovingly at Whoopee in her canary-yellow fisherman's coat, her combat boots, her wild dreadlocks sticking out of her head like accusing fingers, and he just shakes his head. He only loses his cool a little when Whoopee starts coming down the steps two at a time. Her combat boots make a menacing sound as she lets each foot drop like a hammer. Her mouth is about to open when she is halfway down. Ricardo pushes the front door open. He looks back at me and whispers, "Call me when you grow up, María, María." I hear him running down the street. His silk shirt will be ruined by the pouring rain.

Whoopee grabs my hand. "Wanna go for a walk, girlfriend?"

It is many weeks later that I finally ask Uma.

It was the henna tree blossoming outside my window when I was a child in India that I smelled on his skin, the sparrow's song I listened for when he held me close.

Exciting English: I Am a Poet! She Exclaimed

An exclamatory sentence is a strong emotion expressed in words. It begins with a capital letter and ends with an exclamation mark.

These are exclamatory sentences:

Mr. Golden is a musician!

Mr. Golden is a singer!

He thinks I am a good writer!

I wrote a poem!

He wrote music for my words!

He wants to sing it at the last assembly!

Letter to Mami, Not Sent

Querida Mami,

Remember when I was little, and we lived in a little house, in front of a huge ocean, on our little Island? Remember, Mami? You would tell me to sit across from you at the kitchen table, and you would pour me thick orange juice you and I had squeezed ourselves, hot bread we walked to get every morning at 6:00 from the *panadería*, and then you'd make café con leche for yourself, the smell of it so sweet that you said it could raise *los muertos.* Then we would go over our plans for after school. From the time I can remember there was some religion class I had to take at our parish church.

"Hija, I will be waiting for you to take you to Sister María Josefa's catechism class today. Have you memorized your lesson?"

"Yes. But don't make me say it," I would answer. I found the repetitious nature of the pamphlets I had to take home to memorize too simple. It was all "Do you believe in God? Yes, I believe in God. Do you believe in the one, holy, catholic, and apostolic church? Yes, I believe in the one, holy, catholic, and apostolic church." And so on, until the droning of the old nun's monotone voice and the chorus of bored children would be stuck like a record in my head. *¡Sí, sí, sí!* I believe, I believe, I believe!

Mami, you always waited patiently until I said my lesson,

going to the next one only when I had recited the last. It was a standoff — if I played my part just right, the time left before you walked me to school was mine to play or read for pleasure.

And so I learned the trade-off: pay now, fly later.

That is what I feel I am doing repeating the English lessons so I can live in this cold city, Mami. Once I dare to walk outside this little island called the barrio, that is. If you were with me it would be an adventure, like on the day we explored Old San Juan together. We got lost in the old part, but we followed the ancient cobblestone road right down to the ocean and then walked on the beach until we found ourselves back in familiar territory. You said to me, *"Ojo abierto, hija."* Keep your eyes open and you will always find your way back home. Remember, Mami?

Today I will go downtown by myself. I will practice English with real people and try to learn more about the world outside this block so that one day I will stop feeling lost in the world. Maybe I can learn to think of this city as home.

Mami, I think you are learning to live without us. I do not believe you will ever leave your Isla to come live in this cave, as you call the place I now think of as home. You need the tropical sun, and *el azul* much more than I do.

I will not send you this letter so you will not worry that I am getting too triste. I will put it in my poetry notebook and make a poem from it someday.

American Beauty

The minute I step through the electric eye, the drugstore's alarm goes off and several pairs of eyes freeze me inside the cage of their suspicion. I stand on the spiky plastic Welcome mat, waiting for someone to release me, to say "Go on, it is all a mistake." The rotund manager, propelling down the center aisle toward me like a nuclear submarine in his too-tight steel-gray suit, his pudgy finger aimed at me, orders me in a loud voice to come back and empty my purse on the counter. I protest, put my hands up. I have not done anything. But his face — folds of hardened rubbery flesh, mouth curling into a tight smile of scorn, eyes almost slits — tells me to expect no pity. He informs me that he will call security if I do not obey. I turn over my bag on the glass case that displays cheap watches, their plastic faces impassively watching me through safety glass — a jury box of Timex ladies' and men's, alarms ready to go off when I am found guilty, none of them showing the right time.

Without touching any of my things, as if I carried the bubonic plague in my handbag, he inspects its contents, poking around inside with a pen he has pulled out of his pocket, letters scrolled in gold on its side: *We value our customers.* This is what he finds: half a roll of breath mints (tropical flavors), two lipsticks *(Brown Sugar Babe* and *Hot Spice Girl),* hairbrush, pink sunglasses with slightly scratched lenses, envelope with a letter I am still writing to my mother, small mirror in the shape of red lips; two five-dollar bills, three quarters, two dimes, one nickel, and seven pennies — money I was going to spend on beauty products. He takes his time, looking up, raised eyebrows, after tapping each item with his pen. I know he is acting for the security camera. Finally, finding nothing that looks like his merchandise, he looks me over as if I were hiding something in my clothing or maybe hidden deep within my bushy foreign hair. I stand like a statue while he stares. His cheeks begin to quiver a little bit. He rubs his eyes, squints. I turn my five jacket pockets inside out for him; leave their linty insides hanging out. I lean over, grab the hem of my skirt, pretending I am going to lift it up for his inspection. His eyes grow almost round in outrage. He gives me a hateful look, makes a sweeping motion with his plump hand, *Get out of my store.* Case dismissed due to lack of hard evidence; not lack of guilt, his mocking smile tells me. He will get me next time.

He maneuvers his huge body, almost stuck between counter and wall, toward our audience of three customers, his sarcastic smile ugly and mean as the crack on the sidewalk that trips you. *We know she's guilty, right, friends?* He nods as he passes the elderly couple, and nods again at the girl with blonde dreadlocks, who have waited, maybe hoping for the entertainment of their day to end with cops and handcuffs. But they act as if they too feel cheated. The girl walks out without buying anything, tossing back those heavy yellow ropes of hair. The old people return to the magazine they had been flipping through. I watch as the king of these thirteen aisles of beauty products, two of cough and cold, and one of pain relief goes back through his secret panel at the rear wall of his store, to his office behind the two-way mirror.

I put everything slowly back into my bag, taking my time. I sort the coins and put them into the change pocket. I put my makeup in the middle section, zip it up; slide the sunglasses into the outside pocket so they will not be scratched again. I reapply *Brown Sugar Babe* using the mirror on the beauty side of the jewelry, electronics, and beauty aids counter. I run the brush through my hair. It gets stuck in a tough curl and I have to spend a few minutes working it out.

This is what I leave on the glass countertop, above the Timex watches, all telling the wrong time: half a roll of mints (the green one on top broken in three places and a little bit dusty), several strands of coarse black hair I have carefully shaped into a question mark, and a ticket stub from the movie *American Beauty,* which I really didn't like all that much.

Crime in the Barrio

A Poem by María

It begins
with your second last name
gone missing from your mailbox,
school ID, and learner's permit.
It is hard to explain to your relatives
back on the Island.
Your mother says,
you had it
when you left home,
where is it now?
You cannot claim
to have misplaced
your mother's surname.

Your *Abuela* suggests
that you retrace your steps.
Instead, you decide
to just tell everyone
to call you María.
"Just call me María," you say.
It's much simpler this way.

Then, before you know it,
your baby fat is somehow lifted
right from under your very nose.
Where did it go?
Whoever took it
left a couple of bumps
and a few curves
in its place.
You think it may be
someone you know.

Another day
you wake up,
say a few words
and suddenly
you notice, every day
your accent is less thick
than the day before!
Not too long ago
you sounded like this: *I speek
leetle Eenguish.* The next,
you are singing *I can articulate, I can articulate,*
like the eloquent pig Wilbur
in *Charlotte's Web.*

Who is responsible
for these crimes
in the barrio? Who needs
a Puerto Rican accent, a second
last name, or the answer
to the question,
Where are you from?
desperately enough
to break into a basement
apartment, #35½ Market Street,
to steal it
from a fifteen-year-old girl
named María?

She is so subtle, this thief,
that practically
your entire childhood is gone
before you really notice.
You have heard of these strange things
happening to other people,
in exciting places like San Francisco
or Miami, but not
in this barrio,
and not to *you*.

Finally,
you decide to report
these losses to the police.
We recognize the M.O.,
the officer tells you,
*it is a serial thief
who slips through our hands
every time. There is nothing
anyone can do to stop him, yet
it is a matter
of time. Only time will tell
who has taken
your childhood, María.
All we can do is wait and see,
wait and see
if we can catch this thief,
in time, maybe we will.*

To this day
the crimes in the barrio
continue day-by-day,
week-by-week,
and year-by-year.
It is all still a mystery
that may not be solved
in my time.

Love in America

I climb the stairs and stand outside the open door
of Uma's apartment where I can see my friend
kneeling at the window, waiting, for a lover
whose only true passion is his own face in the mirror.

Heartbroken, her tears must sting like hard little grains
of rice, like wedding rice thrown at her face.

The bride wore red, Uma had told me
about a marriage ceremony in her country. *But I will wear
a white dress made of silk and lace when I marry in America.*

Uma's mother sits in her room
reading the letters of her dead husband,
instructions from the grave,
while her daughter kneels at the window waiting,
waiting for what?
For her American prince to rescue her?

Peering over Uma's hunched shoulders
I can see a little child wearing a red dress and a white cap,
playing on the sidewalk, suddenly
spooling out from her mother, almost into the traffic,

then quickly pulled back to safety by her voice,
out and back,
like a yo-yo on an invisible string.

Uma! The mother calls
from the darkened room, the back bedroom
thick with incense, where the faces of dead relatives
speak to Uma's mother from their gilded frames,
telling her how to live in this land of too much freedom,
and what to do about her daughter
who has fallen in love with a boy
who loves only himself. *Uma!*
and Uma is reeled in toward her mother
like a small golden fish, thrust into a sealed world
of sandalwood smoke, of prayer rugs, veils,
and memories.

Uma, I had warned my friend,
he will break your heart. The papi-lindo cannot love
anyone but himself, and all his conquests are little mirrors
he puts up in his room so he can see himself
through each girl's eyes. But when he made a song
of her name *Uma, mi bonita Uma, ven, ven, ven,*
she went to him like an arrow to the target,
up the stairs into his arms she raced,

wearing a blue sari trimmed with tiny silver stars and moons;
her skin of dark honey, scented with the steamed perfume
of rose petals, leaving a trail like a comet's tail
up the stairs, down the hallway,
and into his apartment.

                      Afterward, she brought me
the words he had spoken in her ear: *mi amor, mi vida, Mamacita.*
Words spiced with *adobo,* with *sofrito,* and cooked over an open fire.
I am his life, is this not what it means, María? No, Uma,
to him you are only a new taste on his tongue, the flavor
of new spices — *el sabor del día.*

                          Uma, now kept in
by your mother's fears, you wait each afternoon for the sight
of him, leaping off the bus like an action hero, scaring the pigeons
roosting on the window ledge. But he does not
even glance up, because he is only looking at his own feet
in their fancy Italian shoes, at his own reflection
in the dirty storefront window of the bodega. He is only
lusting after the expensive car that drives by, locked tight
and armored against the dangers of the barrio.

                    Uma, come down the stairs and be my friend.
I will tell you about the *Emancipation Proclamation*, about the Alamo,
the *Louisiana Purchase*, and Eleanor Roosevelt. We will
memorize the names of all the presidents. We will
look at the map together, make lists of cities
we will see someday; cities with names

like songs: Albany, Carmel, Phoenix, San Francisco,
Baton Rouge. Someday we will drive to the capitals
of Europe, the Middle and the Far East without crossing the ocean.
We'll go to Rome, Georgia, to Cairo, Illinois,
and to Paris, Texas —
we will drive a convertible all over the world
and never leave America.

                                        Yet I say nothing.
I cannot speak, nor step into the other world beyond the doorway,
where Uma's mother chants her ancient prayers. Ghosts
are calling out to Uma in her native tongue today,
pulling her to their side.

                                Uma sways back and forth,
as if there were a rubber band attached to her spine. Uma
in her white funeral sari, gathering
her heavy veil of *la tristeza*
over her head, holds tight, tight to the window ledge, stays
on her knees at her window — waiting for the living to call her back
to her American life in Spanish or English
or both?

                                I go back downstairs
and play the best salsa song I know, loud. Loud! I play the tune
that forces your hips and feet to move, even against your will.
I turn up the volume
with the door and windows wide open, sending
the canción up like a spell against death, against sadness, up

and up one flight of stairs: *Come down, Uma,*
let's paint our nails red and practice dancing salsa. I will
teach you some new Spanish words, Uma: ¡Bailar, cantar, vivir!
I say these words like a prayer, a spell against la tristeza.
I chant them like I have heard Uma and her mother do,
adding them to the song already climbing the stairs.
And for once my father is right! Music can
change the world, one heart at a time. *Un corazón, dos, tres,*
then, maybe, the entire universe.

At the threshold of my door
stand Uma and her mother holding hands, black streaks of kohl
running down their cheeks from tears, but trying hard to smile.
"My mother," says Uma, "wonders if you will teach us
how to dance the salsa."
Uma's mother extends one hand to me, and we become
a salsa triangle. "It's all in the hips," I remind them,
"it's all in the hips."

Life Sciences: The Poem As Seen Under the Microscope

Ms. Coronado likes to quote complicated scientific facts
about the beauty and wonder of the natural world
while we take turns at the microscope.
If the DNA of one single human cell were stretched out,
it would measure six and one-half feet! Ms. Coronado
is only five feet tall so she stretches her arms
way above her head to make her point,

Listen to this. The average human being contains
ten to twenty billion, that's billion with a B, people,
miles of DNA! She gets high on these facts,
and the kids make fun of her behind her back,
but she is a popular teacher because she knows
how to make anything interesting, even hours
spent waiting for an amoeba to replicate itself.
Yes! Ms. Coronado is as excited as if we had cloned
a human being. *This is poetry, people, this is a poem*
written by Mother Nature!

The rest of her speech on DNA does not reach my ears
because my lab partner's comment to the tall girl, all angles
and stick-straight hair, a girl made of lines and a plane, hovering
over us, comes to me clear and complete. I cannot move

from my position between them — her perfume
is like a sticky silk web drawing us in. He says to her
over my bent head that I resemble the tadpole floating
in the labeled specimen jar sitting on the shelf
at our station, a bloated, brown little thing.
Reaching for it over my head, the geometric girl
shakes the jar so the small, blind creature
somersaults and cartwheels, then lingers midway
as it falls and rises,
falls and rises,
in its liquid world.

Ms. Coronado places her hands on my shoulders —
she has something to say:
The closer you look at the most ordinary thing,
bee's wing — she interrupts herself — her attention
on my head —

Listen people,
an average human being has about 100,000 individual hairs
on her scalp, she says in wonder, almost to herself.
Look at a cockroach leg or a fruit fly abdomen,
it is a work of art! Look closely,
the closer you look the more beauty you will see.
There is a kaleidoscope of dazzling colors
in an insect's eye, more gorgeous

than a homecoming queen's
rhinestone crown. Each hair
grows about nine inches every year!

Ms. Coronado then asks me for a single hair from my head
that she will place under the microscope;
then she will have everyone in class line up behind me
to see it become poetry.

This will be on the next quiz!
The follicle is like a seed under the ground, it rises
through the dermis and subcutaneous tissue
which is rich in fat and blood vessels, fertile!
The hair shaft is like a little blade of grass
burrowing through the epidermis into the sunlight!
Look close, people.
María has at least 100,000 of these beauties
sprouting from her beautiful head.

Ms. Coronado meant to help me, to save me
from turning into an ugly toad in the minds of my classmates,
but for days I was teased about the tropical rain forest
on my *beautiful* head.

I looked up the parts of a human skin cell —
the words sound like a song in another language:

Dermal papilla, dermal basale, stratum spinosum, stratum
corneum, epidermis, dermis . . . and . . .
as I look at the illustration
of a cross section of skin — I have a Ms. Coronado moment:
People, listen to this: We are all made up of the same thing
under our *epidermis.*

English Declaration:
I Am the Subject of a Sentence

The subject of a sentence (underlined) is the part talked about.
"María, please read some of your poems to our class."
(I do not say this aloud: Oh no, Mr. Golden. I am afraid
of what my classmates will think. I will be the subject
of their insults.)
They will say:

The <u>girl</u> thinks she is an American.

<u>María</u> thinks she is good in English.

The <u>girl</u> can't write.

<u>María</u> speaks with an accent.

The <u>poems</u> have an accent

just like María's.

The <u>poems</u> are ugly.

<u>She</u> is ugly.

The <u>teacher</u> likes María.

<u>María</u> is the teacher's little pet.

<u>He</u> will say to the class, you are fools.

The <u>class</u> will laugh at María. They will

hate her

and her poem.

Find the subject in these sentences:

Their laughter
is what María Alegre fears,
also their mockery
of her still-thick accent,
and their teasing
about her poetry.
She will turn into María Triste.
They are silent.
They are waiting
for her to read her poems.
When she finishes reading
she is amazed by what she hears.
Applause!
People are looking at her
in a different way

"In our society poets are often ignored," Mr. Golden says,
"and almost always poor. Yet they are never unemployed.
They are always at work, on the job,
looking for the truth.
María, you are a poet,"
Mr. Golden declares.

After School, I Hear Whoopee

yelling, *I love the rain! I love the rain! María, come out and play!*
Out of the top half of my basement window, I watch her running down our block, a manic look of happiness on her face.
She loves it when it rains hard. The world belongs only to the
crazy people then, she says. She is splashing water on purpose,
jumping into puddles.

I knew that in a minute she would be dragging me into
her latest craziness. Maybe we'll walk to the deserted play-
ground, slide and swing in the rain, or maybe we will take a
bus to the mall and annoy people by walking around dripping
wet, her high-top sneakers squeaking. Or maybe I will ask her
to stay in with me tonight and just be quiet. I will tell her
about being called a frog in class today, and about making a
poem from a single strand of hair. Whoopee will offer to brush
my hair. She will teach me how to twist it and turn it into
braids and dreadlocks. We will look up magic spells so we can
turn some people at school into warty frogs. And although
we will not find a spell to turn enemies into frogs, we learn
that frogs were considered symbols of good luck in ancient
Egypt. They were embalmed and kept around the house.
There is a picture of a tiny frog mummy that makes
Whoopee decide we should make frog mummies out of
papier-mâché to give as party favors at Ms. Coronado's annual
fiesta. She will love the idea of frog mummies and maybe,

Whoopee suggests, maybe even a frog piñata filled with chocolate frogs!

My friend Whoopee, who doesn't believe she is beautiful herself, will make me laugh and look at myself in the mirror while she transforms me from María Triste into María Alegre. Whoopee is magic.

"Silent Night" in Spanish and Two Glamour Shots of My Island Grandmother

Regalos de Navidad. As a Christmas gift, my mother sends me a CD of El Gran Combo featuring "Silent Night" in Spanish, *"Noche de paz, noche de amor."* This will not be a night of peace in the barrio, Mami. All around me on this Christmas Eve, the night begins to fill with the hot sounds of music from stereos and radios, hot enough to melt the ice and snow that has accumulated this long winter keeping us sealed in our separate spaces. All our neighbors' doors will be open tonight in our building. Papi is rehearsing his high-volume version of *"Feliz Navidad"* in his room. The wall we share is vibrating just a little as he kicks up the tempo.

My grandmother sends me two pictures of herself when she was about my age. In one photo, Abuela is standing under a graceful palm tree. It is a moonlit night on the beach. The sea in the background is smooth as a black mirror. The palm tree bends toward her like a skinny admirer with wild hair. She is wearing a shiny black evening gown, hoop earrings peep through her dark curls. She is holding a large hibiscus blossom in her hand. Her smile is mine. I see my eyes on her face. But I will be taller. In the other picture, her chin is resting on her hands as she gazes dreamily beyond the camera, looking like a movie star of the past. She always told me that

I looked exactly like she did at fifteen, but our resemblance is less obvious in the close-up photograph. I may never pose in a glamorous evening gown under a perfect silver moon, Abuela, nor on the seashore of a tropical island, in a perfect black-and-white world, but I will have a *Noche de paz, noche de amor* among my new friends here tonight.

Math Class: Sharing the Pie

The circle, y'all should know,
is a universal shape. You find circles everywhere
in this world of ours, and indeed, in our entire universe.
Just take a look around, says Mr. C. in his soft voice
laced with a thick Southern accent
that makes the girls giggle — they like to say the *C*
stands for "cute" — and the boys
want to sound like him, *y'all.*

Y'all hush and listen to me.
Circles are everywhere. Can anyone name
the circle that you live on, the circle that warms
and lights our days, the circle that illuminates
our nights? He turns to the chalkboard
and draws a circle. *Let us look*
at a shape y'all will recognize, the good ole pie,
it's what taught you how to share
in grade-school, folks, how to be fair
to one another by using fractions. Remember?
Mr. C. faces us and does a silly little tap dance
while reciting:
One-half for you, one-half for me,
or if there are more than two, one-third for him, one-third
for me, one-third for Sue.

85

We all groan when Mr. C.
makes up his silly math rhymes. We put our heads down
on our desks when he sings *and* dances.

Mr. C. is tall
and built like a football player. Yet he speaks softly
and seems shy. Sometimes
he looks out at the gray sky and the slush-covered
streets from his classroom window and I know
that he is missing the Martian-red ground,
the green woods, and the hot sun
of his native Georgia. Maybe he is thinking
of juicy peaches, of red-orange pumpkins
like the setting sun, and of a silver moon
over a fishing pond deep in the green woods
where a boy could sit under a weeping willow tree
and think of numbers:
the dozens of fish in the water,
the hundreds of rabbits in the bushes,
the thousands of birds navigating
by the sun and moon,
heading south in the fall and north
in the spring. Mr. C. has told us that hummingbirds
beat their wings seventy-eight times a second and are only
about two and one-half inches long,
yet they will fly hundreds of miles
as they migrate from one continent to the next

in search of the sweet nectar of hibiscus and poppy,
of red flowers that depend on the cycle
of pollination for their own survival. *It is all
part of the circle, folks. Who remembers
the formula for distance?*

Bees can collect pollen
from more than 500 flowers
in one single trip. (I imagine him chasing a bee
from flower to flower, counting, 497, 498, 499, 500!)
And did we know that a falcon can dive
at one hundred miles per hour when pursuing prey?
*Numbers, shapes, animals, the food chain, all go around
in a circle called life. Come on, y'all, wake up!* Mr. C.
informs us that he has known schools of fish that look livelier
than we do at this time of the afternoon. *Math gets harder
the later in the day it is, I know. Wake up,
or I'll tell you another fishing story.*

No, no! We all yell, pretending
we hate his stories about growing up in the country,
all of them math problems for us to solve.

We are his last group of the day.
He meets us when it's already almost dark
outside, when he has to work as hard as an actor

on the stage to make numbers dance and sing for us.

He looks at the class waiting
for us to tell him about circles in our lives and sighs,
only ten more minutes of math class left. He zeroes in
on me. *What do you have to say
about circles, María?* I am suddenly feeling timid,
and just shake my head.

In my mind I say: Circles are the shape
I drew with my toe on the sands of la playa,
where my mother took me every day to play.
We made up a game of finding treasures
the sea gave away after a tide. She taught me
shapes and colors this way, by looking for *los tesoros del mar*
under the yellow ball of the tropical sun
shining on our little Island, a dot
on the globe of the world. These are the circles
in my world, Mr. C.

I understand, María, says Mr. C.,
glancing out the window at the snow
covering everything now —
there is no green in our world today, *no hay verde,*
the color of hope, the color of home,
no colors anywhere. *I understand,* Mr. C. repeats,

although I have not spoken a word.

What does he understand? Why I do not always
choose to talk in class? Does he understand
what it is like to sound different from others
so that some people will look at you as if you are
from another planet, and others will laugh
as if everything you say is a joke? I think
he understands missing the colors, sounds,
and the smells of the place where you will not
be asked where you are from the minute
you open your mouth to speak. I think Mr. C.
understands how I feel on this cold winter day
that looks like somebody threw a white bedsheet
over the entire city, no colors anywhere.

       The bell rings,
but even as we leave his room, he is still
at the chalkboard, lost in his dream
of circles. Is he thinking about the way the moon
and the stars guide the birds to the flowers, and the flowers
draw the bees, and the fish rise to the surface
to warm themselves in the summer sun, and the boy
goes to the pond to think of numbers, and somehow
all of it leads him to us?

       Later, at home,
as I memorize the formula for finding the area

of a circle — pi times the radius squared — I think
of Mr. C. dividing the pie into halves, and fourths,
and eighths, and sixteenths, and more, trying to teach us
in the best way he knows, how everything
is connected, how straight lines can be shaped
into a circle, and a circle transformed
into the pie of his dreams, the pie
he will somehow find a way
for all of us to share.

Abuela's Winter Visit

In February, my mother sent her mother, my abuela, to check up on me because she and Papi were not talking. Poor Abuela hates the cold, and she hates our dark basement apartment. So I painted the tiny room we call our guest room white; everything in it got a whitewash, including the twin bed Papi bought from a tenant. He gave me money and I bought white sheets. It was brilliant, I thought. White on white. When you opened the door and turned on the overhead light (one hundred watts), it was as if a flashbulb had gone off in front of your face. Abuela would not be able to say that she had to walk around like a bat in a cave, finding her way by radar in our apartment.

La Abuela's Island Lament: A One-Act Play

My grandmother comes into the kitchen where I am sitting down at the table reading a magazine. It is a dark winter day. Rain and sleet have been predicted. Abuela shakes her head as she looks out the window of our basement apartment. All the feet that pass by are wearing boots. She pours herself a cup of coffee and sits down across from me. She sighs as if her heart is breaking. She shivers and pulls her sweater around her shoulders. Papi comes in whistling. It is his day off. He will spend it with friends he knew from when he was a boy in the barrio. They will go to the park, even if it's raining or cold, and talk about the good times they had as children.

Abuela says, shivering, "María, let me tell you about my Island in the sun. The place where I was born. A paradise."

Papi, frowning as he struggles to put on his boots, says, "I know, I know your paradise. I lived there once, remember? In San Juan, I couldn't see the sun behind the buildings. I'll take the island of Manhattan anytime, if what I want is a paradise made of concrete."

Abuela, ignoring him, tapping my hand as she speaks.

I am trying to stay out of it, hiding behind my magazine: "*Ay, bendita hija.* When I was growing up on my Island, everyone treated each other nicely, like family. We shared what we had, and if you were poor, your neighbors helped you. *La familia, los amigos, el amor,* that's what mattered. People were not always angry; people were not cold like they are here in this cold place, these are cold people . . . the sun shines every day on my Island."

Papi, sounding angry: "The familia on your Island made fun of me, called me *el gringo* because my Spanish sounded funny to their ears. They laughed when I complained that the mosquitoes were eating me alive. Fresh American blood, they joked, to fatten up our hungry bugs. I couldn't wait to come home to *my* country where people understand what I say, and the mosquitoes treat everyone the same."

Abuela, paying no attention to Papi, moving her chair closer to mine: "When I was your age on my Island there was no crime, no violence, no drugs. The children respected the adults. We obeyed the teachers, the priests, the Pope, the governor, and our parents. The sun shines every day. On my Island . . ."

Papi: "I once had my wallet stolen in the plaza of your pueblo, Señora. I used to watch the news in the bedroom, while everyone else sat hypnotized by the romantic telenovelas in the living room. On my screen was the same world I see on our TV here: drugs, guns, angry people, and violence. Only difference — the bad news was in Spanish."

Abuela, not listening. Looking into her cup as if she were watching a movie: "The sun shines every day. On my Island . . ."

Papi, in a mocking tone of voice: "The sun shines every day, that's true. While I was unhappy, missing my friends here, while I was lonely, the sun shone every day and it was 110 degrees in the shade."

Abuela: "On my Island . . ."

Before she can finish her sentence, the lights flash on and off, and then we hear the gasping sounds of electrical things shutting down and darkness. A roll of thunder shakes the glass window. We hear the sound of feet running on the sidewalk above our heads. Abuela gets a candle from a kitchen drawer, places it on the table, and lights it. There is another roll of thunder and the sound of pouring rain. I hear Papi opening the pantry door to get his flashlight. The telephone begins to ring. I run to get it, grateful that it has interrupted a culture clash I have been hearing all of my life. It is the old battle between Island Puerto Rican and mainland Puerto Rican. It is what finally drove my parents apart.

On the telephone, I hear Doña Segura's shaky voice asking me in Spanish if Papi can come see about a smell like gas in her apartment. Everyone else is away for the day. She is blind. She does not even know that it is dark. Abuela nods. I know she will go stay with Doña Segura.

Papi, already dressed for his day of freedom, listens to me tell Doña Segura that she will be right up. I look at my father by the light of the candle. Both of us sigh in unison, a big, deep, melodramatic, Puerto Rican sigh. Abuela's candle is blown out by our breath. Then there is the sound of three people laughing together in the dark.

Who Are You Today, María?

Abuela knocks on my bedroom door. She has come to my room this morning to watch me choose my outfit for Who You Are Day at school. This is a day when we are allowed to dress in clothes that we think tell the world who we really are. (Within reason, our principal warned — no extremes will be tolerated. I hope that her definition of the word *extreme* is the same as my friend Whoopee's. Nothing that she will put on this morning has ever been seen on this planet, much less at school.)

Abuela makes herself comfortable on my bed as I put on my costume of myself made up of pieces of my life. I thought about my Who You Are Day outfit a lot. Mr. Golden told us in English class to think about our choices: are you going to walk around as a joke or as a poem? I have a suspicion that our teachers have allowed us this chance to dress up as ourselves for a reason. Our school is already a united nations, a carnival, and a parade all at once. There are students from dozens of different countries, and we do not always get along. Most of us are too shy to talk to others outside our little circles, and so misunderstandings come up. The principal has tried almost everything. The Who You Are Day is another of her crazy ideas to get us to communicate. In each of my classes, the teacher said, let us know something about what has made you who you are by what you wear to school tomorrow. It all sounds like a conspiracy to me. But I like dressing up so I do not complain like the boys have been doing. Most of them hate the idea!

Abuela looks at my choices hanging on the door and shakes her head, smiling, like she did when we went to see *Cats*. It is a smile that says, I do not understand, but if it is important to María, I will bear it the best I can. She is elegant even at 7:00 A.M. in her embroidered silk robe and red velvet slippers. She has wrapped a shawl over her shoulders because she is always cold in our *cueva,* as she calls the apartment. The shawl was handmade by her mother and it is Abuela's most prized possession. As a little girl, I liked to put it over my head because the pattern of sequins made a night sky full of stars and because it smelled like Abuela.

Abuela sips from her cup of café con leche as she watches me.

I feel a little strange about being in my underwear in front of her and go in my closet with my choices, which are:

My mother's red skirt that she wore when she had a part in a musical play on the Island. I have played dress-up with it since I was five years old, but it finally fits me perfectly. It is the kind of skirt that opens like an umbrella when you turn in circles.

A top I sewed together from an old sari Uma's mother was going to throw away. It is turquoise blue with silver edges.

And finally, over my sari, I will wear my father's sharkskin suit jacket — it's big on me but I can roll up the sleeves. It is what he likes to wear when he sings at rent parties. Under the light, it changes colors and seems to come alive as the design shifts and moves. Papi says it is great for dancing; you don't even need a partner.

And finally, tall platform shoes we found buried deep in Whoopee's closet, circa 1974, she told me. Whoopee collects antique shoes to go with her science fiction outfits. It is a fashion statement; she will tell anyone who asks. No one knows what the statement means, and that is just fine with Whoopee.

When I part the clothes in my closet and come out like an actor in a play, Abuela's eyes open wide. Before she can say anything, I point to each piece of my outfit and say a name: Mami, Papi, Uma, and Whoopee.

Abuela's face changes as she begins to understand the meaning of my fashion statement.

"Ahora sé quién eres, María, y quién puedes ser, si quieres. Ven acá, mi amor."

Abuela says that she knows who I am and who I may be if I choose. I have heard those words before but I don't remember when or where. Abuela embraces me and kisses my face several times. This is a Puerto Rican thing. It goes on for a while. I close my eyes to wait it out and I suddenly inhale a familiar scent. When I open my eyes, I see a starry sky. Abuela has put her shawl over my head.

"*Algo mío para tu día de ser quien eres, mi hija,*" she tells me. *Something of mine for your day of being who you are.* She is letting me borrow her mother's beautiful shawl!

All day at school, I feel elegant. Whenever anyone tries to make fun of my costume, I think of the words my grandmother quoted to me: *I know who you are and who you may be if you choose.* And when I go into Mr. Golden's class and his eyes ask me, *Who are you today, María?* I will say by the way I walk in, head held high, that today I am a poem.

Translating Abuela:
I Know Who I Am

When Abuela went home, she left behind a black notebook in which she wrote her *pensamientos,* her thoughts, each night before going to bed. When I called her to ask if she wanted me to mail it to her, she said I should keep it and translate it — to practice my Spanish. Mami laughed when I told her about this. Abuela had left her journals around for *her* to read when she was my age. It is Abuela's way of letting us know who she really is, and what she thinks is important. On the hardback cover of all her notebooks she had quotations from books she had read.

Translating Abuela's Journal: The Ice Age

My María put me in a room sterilized and painted in shades of white like a hospital. The bed is hard and the sheets always feel so stiff, I think they have just been taken out of their store packages, never having been shaped and molded by any human body. I have to take a deep breath and brace myself as I plunge under the icy *sábanas*. I know that she is trying hard to make me comfortable, but how I long to be in my own bed that cocoons me in its soft and yielding middle as it did my own mother before me, and to throw my *ventanas* open to the breezes of my Island and to the sound of the *coquíes*. I must remember to ask my *comadre* to make sure that no creatures get in my house while I am away; I always hate coming home to sweep up the dried-up little corpses of lizards and the countless spiders and mosquitoes that insist on coming into the house to die.

Translating Abuela's Journal:
After I Take Her to the Museum and the Theater

I would rather look through a family album of photographs, even old and faded ones, than at a museum full of pictures of lonely mountains and skeletal trees. My granddaughter wants me to see how educated and cultured she is becoming. One day María and I spent three hours doing just that! Mr. Ansel Adams must have really liked being out in the cold by himself, that is all I could find to say about him. After we had crawled up from one level to another of the museum to see mountains, more mountains, trees, more trees, rivers, creeks, puddles, and all of it in black and white! Not one single human face in the entire exhibit. And this Guggenheim building an evil architect had designed in the shape of a nautilus shell nearly caused me to have a thrombosis. You had to be a slimy snail to enjoy going around and around and up and up.

Another time, we went to see a play called *Gatos.* I confess only to you, Dear Diary — I find it impossible to be moved by a female cat singing her heart out about a hard life, and this *after* having been run over by a car. Who can believe that? But my María Alegre, my darling *nieta,* loved the actors in their feline costumes and was thrilled when they ran out into the dark theater flashing their eyes like little headlights. And she was moved to tears by their songs. I saw her wiping away tears while that scraggly *gata* wailed about her tragic life and early demise. I must admit that I was probably missing the symbolism that made my granddaughter weep because of my limited understanding of the English language. But still, to cry over gatos? And it is not as if I had not been exposed to culture in my time. On the Island, my mamá María and my papá José took us to the theaters to see some wonderful productions. Many of the plays were the works of *our own* young playwrights, as well as classics from Latin America and Spain. The tears shed there by the audience were for the end of love, for death, for *la patria* — important matters of the heart and soul. Maybe I am just an old abuela from the Island. Maybe I should wear my hair in a bun and dress only in black clothes. Let them call me a *jíbara,* if they want. I will never shed a tear for a cat, no matter how tragic their lives may be. How ridiculous.

Translating Abuela's Journal: The Final Entry

On the last page of the *libreta* she left for me to read Abuela had written a line from *Don Quixote* that she had translated to English: *I know who I am and who I may be if I choose.*

English: I Am the Simple Subject

"After school, you and I will work together on your poems, María," Mr. Golden tells me after class. "There is an old saying that goes like this: Success is the best revenge."

"But, Mr. Golden, I do not yet have all the words I need to make poems."

"Take words where you find them, María. Do what you have to do to keep writing your stories and poems, María," Mr. Golden said, "just as I must do what I need to do to keep singing my songs.

"You have a gift; it is the gift of metaphor. María, go out and see if you can see the universe in a grain of sand. Here, take this." He hands me a book of poems in both Spanish and English. It is Pablo Neruda's *Elementary Odes, Odas elementales.*

I thank him in words, but answer him only in my thoughts: Mr. Golden *está bien*, I believe you, since you declare that I am a poet, since it is imperative that I be a poet, I will be a poet. But how do I become a poet? I live in a small world with few exclamation points and many question marks. Will I have to look for the universe in the cement and the concrete of my street? Will I have to look for metaphors in the plaster of the walls of our home, in the sad notes of my father's guitar late at night, in the sad golden eyes of my friend Uma? Will I have to find poetry in Whoopee's red sneakers and her Tarzan song? Will I have to make poems out of common, ordinary things no one except me cares about? No one will want to read my poems, Mr. Golden.

But later, sitting at my desk by the window where I can see the feet passing by, the shoes and the socks of people whose lives and secret dreams I try to imagine as I do my homework, I open the book and read Pablo Neruda's poem titles . . . and my heart jumps like a small frog inside my chest! Yes, I see that I will have to make poems out of blue socks, red tomatoes, yellow birds, onions, lemons, cats, artichokes, elephants, panthers; about things that work just fine, like a watch in the night (the minutes falling like leaves from a tree, says Pablo Neruda), and also about broken things. And maybe someone in my future, someone who needs to know if her world is too small to write about will hold my book in her hands and read my *poemas elementales,* and say yes, I can be a poet too. —

Gracias, Mr. Golden.

My Papi-Azul and Me, the Brown Iguana

My father emerges
from our basement apartment
in his blue workman's uniform.
He is all in blue.
Blue workman's pants, blue shirt, blue
Yankees cap. My father is a cloudy sky,
a storm at sea. Blue father,
my *Papi-Azul.*
"María, whatcha doin'?"
"*Nada,*" I say. "I am lounging
like a small brown iguana
in the first warm day of spring."
"*Bueno,*" he says, "I won't be back
for *la cena* tonight. I'll eat
at la bodega."
"I am a small brown iguana," I say,
"warming myself in the sun."
But he is not listening.
He has places to go,
people to see.

Rent Party

It is getting warmer now, and our duties are lighter. The fire-breathing monster in the basement is hibernating, and the residents of our building are resigned to suffering through another sweltering summer with windows thrown open to catch the rare city breeze. My father is completely at home on this street, in this setting. He wants to be King of the Barrio, although his throne room is in the basement. He rules because he has the master key and he has the toolbox and he has the songs and the voice and the heart.

On weekends, Papi can usually be found on one of the higher floors, a popular guest with his guitar and repertoire of old songs fresh from La Isla. Usually he leaves me a note telling me where he will be that night — which is often at a "rent party." There is always one in progress on a Saturday night in our building: for a few dollars or a song, Doña so-and-so will provide her living room as a dance floor and make *mondongo, asopao,* or homemade *pasteles,* or whatever Island recipe she knows will loosen your wallet and your homesick tears. And, *¡fiesta!,* she will make rent that month. My father is always invited for his musical accompaniment to their sad midnight songs about an Island some of them have never visited or, like my father, a place they do not call home by choice.

There Go the Barrio Women

Barrio women with the strong, muscular legs I watch pass by through the grille at the top of my basement window march themselves like warriors to the front lines, to their jobs in factories all day, then return to their tiny, cold apartments to work some more, taking care of children and their mostly absent husbands — many of the younger men of the barrio are the mercenary troops in this war — making their brief appearances, leaving a swollen belly here and there. They also party as hard as they work. On weekends, the ceiling of our basement apartment trembles above me. Bits of plaster sometimes rain on my head from the feet pounding out their *cumbias, pachangas,* and mambos, as they work *"la lucha"* out of their systems. Will I become as strong as the barrio women? *Creo que sí.* Will I dance my troubles away after a week of hard work? *Claro que sí.* But I want my *luchas* to be the ones *I* choose.

My Mother, the Rain. El Fin

It is April of the first year of my American life when my mother finally comes to visit us.

I sit on the top step as the hour of Mami's arrival approaches. It is a warm evening and the sidewalk is crowded with people sitting on folding chairs, mainly women and children. The noise level rises steadily as radios are brought out and people adjust the volume of their voices to compete with the music. I like to listen to the old women talking about their previous incarnations as island puertorriqueñas. Some of them talk only about how much better life was en La Isla: the people were kinder, the weather perfect, the *arroz y habichuelas, plátanos, pollo frito, café con leche, maví* — talking about the food as cooked by their mamás makes some of them stand up on the top step like poets inspired to recite verses to their native land. *¡Ay, ay, ay, bendito!* But someone always points out that beautiful scenery did not fill empty stomachs. *"¡Hay que comer, hijas!"* One has to eat. No one disagrees with this opinion.

I listen, but do not speak. I know that even though I am in their circle, I am not really a part of the powerful barrio women's society yet. They all know that a different kind of hunger brought my father and me to this island in the city, but one more difficult to satisfy than food hunger or money hunger. My father missed the barrio of his younger days; he had to come home, and I wanted an American education. The barrio women, Pura, Isabel, Clara, Cordelia, Concepción, and their new American children, Lynette Gómez, Janice García, Joey Flores, and all the ones that would come after them, were new here like me — and the new barrio dwellers would have to take on new colors to survive. I know this from having studied island chameleons as a child, the talented little lizards always come back to their original colors when they feel safe in their environment. I can see the women in front of this building in our American city are not that different from the women in their porch rockers on the Island.

In the late afternoons and sometimes even at night, I sit on our building's front stoop to enjoy their Spanglish poetry slam and gossip sessions. As I wait for Papi's car to drive up, with my mother in the passenger seat, I dream that Mami will now join me on these old steps. Here I will teach her about my new American life, and she will decide to stay with us.

Papi pulls up in front of our building in his sleek parrot-green Thunderbird. There are wolf whistles and wild clapping from some of the women. The car has barely stopped moving when several children wearing only underwear or shorts climb on its shiny hood. Papi is wearing a new red shirt and black pants and his hair and mustache are blue-black from the Nice 'n Easy color I put in it. He is not the same man as he is in his blue workman's uniform. He is not strutting as usual, and I can tell something is wrong. He is trying hard to be a gentle-man, but after he opens the passenger door for Mami — she swings her tanned legs out of the car with the grace of a dancer; her movements are a ballet — he slams it hard. He pulls away too fast, wheels squealing. Something has happened between them. But I do not want to think about problems just then, I just want to run into my mother's arms.

It has been a whole year since I have seen her! I notice that Mami's face is as perfectly made up as that of a model in a glossy magazine. Her flawless complexion and athletic body are the result of a lot of hard work. She always said to me: *María, you do not need to be rich to be healthy and look good; money buys you dermatologists, orthodontists, and hair stylists, but exercise is free, and a person who takes care of her looks tells the world that she respects herself.* I had put on my happy mouth today, just for her — Berry Berry Red, a new shade, and I had curled my hair. Alegre, Alegre. Call me María Alegre!

Mami gives me a big, big smile and opens her arms for me to come to her. I feel like I am in a play. I feel the eyes of the barrio women behind me. They are watching me to see who I really am. Am I an Island woman or a barrio woman? Can I be both?

I see Mami's eyes sweep over the scene on the stoop leading to our building. I know she disapproves of this society, definitely not the kind of club that she wants me to join. I know what she sees: The old women with legs spread wide to cool themselves blatantly staring at us, the sweaty children running up and "tagging" Papi's car, leaving dirty handprints on its gemstone finish, while he is trying to maneuver into a tight spot. The same things that normally make up my front-yard world, one I thought I was finally beginning to understand, now embarrass me. I imagine seeing the crude scene through Mami's eyes. Her eyes that open every morning to the turquoise sea, *un cielo azul,* to her ears that hear Spanish spoken in a completely different way than the way we use the mother tongue here.

I run to hug her, to protect her.

I will get her past the evil tongues, *las malas lenguas.* And once we are safely inside our little basement apartment that I have scrubbed and cleaned for her visit, she will see that I have made a true casa for Papi and me in the middle of this foreign place, this cold city.

There are murmurs and giggles from some of the barrio women as they watch the elegantly dressed Mami and me walk down into our apartment, our arms around each other. She is wearing an ivory suit of some soft material, perhaps silk, and big, dark, and matching soft brown leather shoulder bag and pumps. Very island Puerto Rican dressy. And very unusual attire on our block, where men walk around in their T-shirts and cut-off shorts at this time of year and women wear as little as they can. It is a matter of surviving the heat in the city.

"*Mira,* the fancy *pájara* is about to inspect her golden cage," Clara points her nose at my mother, speaking loudly enough for us to hear. Some of the children take up the chant, "Pájara, pájara. Pretty bird, pretty bird."

There is unabashed laughter in the circle. I am ready to defend my mother against their rudeness, though I know I would also be condemning myself to their persecution. They are enjoying *el gufeo*, goofing off, Spanglish style. The catcalls and verbal abuse inflicted on the ones who act snobbish around the gate keepers, as Whoopee calls the old women who sit, watch, and comment on everything that happens on our street, are a familiar part of daily life here. Everyone gets humbled by the *viejas*. They teach the game to the younger ones. But el gufeo is not what I wanted Mami to endure on her first minutes in the barrio. At the risk of my own future, I start to tell them to shut up. But Mami squeezes my hand. I look at her calm face, the cool smile that says, *Do not worry. They cannot touch me.* She leads me slowly past them, bearing with grace their laughter and sarcastic gazes. Some of the younger women clap and whistle as if we were putting on a show for them. The old ones look at us in solemn silence. They were once Island women themselves. They know. Sometimes you are born to be one or the other. Sometimes you can cross over.

I *know* the viejas respect my mother's self-control. I lead Mami by the hand down the steps and into #35½ Market Street, our apartment under the ground. We sit close together on the sofa, not saying anything for a few moments. She had asked Papi for a few hours alone with me. She looks around and then leans over to switch on a lamp. I had forgotten that she couldn't stand dim rooms.

We talk about everything for a while. I can tell that she has something on her mind. But I already know she will not stay. It is obvious that this is a visit. It is only when I offer to show her the little white painted room where Abuela had stayed — I had painted it yellow for Mami — she begins to cry.

She admits that she will not be moving in with us. She has fallen in love with another man, a fellow teacher. Did I remember him? Julio? He teaches history at her school. They are in love. She is asking Papi for a divorce. He had been furious when she told him on the way here.

"María, I thought that he would have gotten used to the idea of our separation by now. I believed we could present this to you like civilized people. *Pero tu papi no cambia.* He is the same papi-lindo I met in high school. He expects to be loved unconditionally by everyone — at least by all the women. It has always been this way with him."

I just shake my head. Both my parents are wrong about each other. It is breaking my heart to hear her speak about my father this way. I decide it is better for me to be silent for now. I had learned long ago that fights between my parents could not be resolved by me. If I defend him, she will be hurt, and vice versa.

She asks me to return to the Island and live with her

and Julio. She says this is not the place she had imagined for me.

My head hurts. My chest hurts. I smell her familiar perfume, I listen to her voice until she says all she has come to say. Then I show her my little cavelike bedroom. I show her how I can feel the giant boiler, the Dragon, in the winter by putting my ear to the wall.

When we come back to the living room, she is calmer. I let her sit at my desk under the street-level window where I watch legs go by when I do my homework, when I write to her. I read her some of my Instant Histories. I tell her about Uma, Papi-lindo, about Doña Segura, and about my best friend, Whoopee Dominguez, who had interested me even before she stuck her face at my window because of her combat boots and her powerful voice. Mami holds my poetry notebook in her hands a long time and then she presses it to her heart in a very dramatic, Puerto Rican–telenovela sort of way.

"*Eres una poeta,* María," she said.

"In three languages, Mami. I am a trilingual poet."

"Three languages? English, Spanish . . ."

"And Spanglish." I read her my instant history of Whoopee.

Mami laughs at my third language. "You are good at Spanglish, María. You know it's what your father spoke when he was growing up."

"And what he speaks again now, Mami."

Then she began to cry again. "It is like we are from two different countries, hija. Both Puerto Ricans, but we have never spoken the same language."

I know what that feels like. There are many ways to be a foreigner. I spend the evening comforting my mother.

It is dark outside when we hear the turning of a key in the front door. Papi has apparently stumbled on his way in and is calling out my name in a slurry, thick voice I hardly recognize. He is drunk. He never comes home drunk, or if he does, he makes sure I do not know about it. Though sometimes I have found the evidence of a hangover in our kitchen sink — the glass crusted with dry grains of Alka-Seltzer, the bottle of aspirin left on the table, a bag of ice in the freezer. But I have never seen him in the crashing, stumbling, word-slurring condition he is in this night. He stands in the doorway, his arms outstretched, head lolling around like a puppet's. My shame is complete. My mother will now think that our lives are a disgrace. My father looks like any barrio derelict: circles of sweat under his arms, a flush darkening his face, and the sarcastic grin of any ordinary drunkard as he looks mockingly at Mami and me sitting on the sofa, a book of poetry between us. He is very angry and very *borracho*.

"Mother and hija reunited at last. We are a familia again! At least for a few minutes, *¿verdad, querida?* Did you tell our María Alegre you plan to *abandonarnos?*"

Mami stands up, extending her hand with its manicured

fingernails and tasteful gold bracelet toward my father who stares at her with an expression of utter disdain, and then he turns his head away and vomits on the hallway floor. We barely manage to grab him under his flopping arms and drag him to his bed. He begins snoring almost immediately. Sick at the sight of him, his disgrace now complete in my eyes, I start to leave his room. But Mami does not follow me out of the dark, man-smelling place where my father smokes his cigars and reads *La Prensa,* stacking papers and magazines around his bed as if he were building a wall of moldy newsprint around himself. I turn to see a strange scene: Mami tenderly tucking a blanket around my unconscious father, then pausing to look intently at his sad face. I see my mother gaze at him with tenderness, and I am confused again by it all. "Hija," I hear him moan before I close the door to his room behind us. Is he calling for me because he is afraid I will leave him too? His voice sounds like that of a drowning man. What would happen to him if I left him alone with the Dragon in the basement? I will not leave him.

Mami will not stay. The man she loves now, Julio the historian, who takes her to museums, was due to pick her up here, in front of our building. They are going to spend a day or two in New York, going to museums of course, and then they will return to the Island. Listening to her plans makes me feel as if a small black bird called el pájaro triste has just awakened inside my chest. It wants to be set free, to come out through my eyes as tears, through my mouth as angry words, black feathers that would shock and frighten my soft-spoken, well-dressed island mother. But I keep la tristeza inside me.

I let her talk. She keeps looking at her watch. She asks me again if I am *completamente segura,* certain without any doubt that I want to stay in *this* place. I just nod. How can I explain to her that what she called *this place* with so much disdain is now *mi isla, mi casa.* Also, I have responsibilities: I have to make sure the tenants of our building get their leaks fixed, their apartments painted, their favorite songs sung by Papi. El Súper needs his assistant. Maybe, *quizás,* I say when she asks me if I will meet her and Julio at the Museo del Barrio. I do not tell her that I am not ready for outings with her and her future husband yet. *Sí, claro,* I will call her *mañana.*

I say good-bye to Mami in the street, *adiós, Mami, adiós.* The front stoop is now populated by the quieter night people. The old gate keepers who had worn themselves out during the day are now fanning themselves quietly, watching over the tired-to-the-bone single mothers holding sleepy babies on their laps.

She says in her most tender Mami-voice, her *azúcar*-coated-voice, "Write, María. Mi María Alegre, call if you need me."

I say, "Yes, yes. Sí, Mami," in my little María voice. Neither triste nor alegre. Call me María. Just María. I kiss her cheek and she holds me close for a moment. But I knew her eyes were looking past me, looking for her future to drive up. Julio. El amor. Spanish is so beautiful. A perfect language for love. El amor. A few raindrops fall on us.

A black car pulls up. Mami waves to me as she hurries to a big Eldorado, a rental, already bearing the evidence of dirty little hands all over it. It is starting to sprinkle. The old women are folding their aluminum chairs and hurrying inside. I hear windows being raised, voices calling out "*¡Qué lluvia!*" It is not a complaint. The smell of rain is a promise of a cooler night for my neighbors and for me. The rain, la lluvia, is a blessing on the long hot nights of this barrio. Tonight, I will wait until the street is wet, shiny, and transformed before going in to begin writing the letter to my mother, the one I want her to find waiting for her when she returns to the Island. I will tell her I am glad that she is happy. I will tell her not to worry about Papi and me. We *are* home.

My Father Changing Colors

Papi sometimes goes around the barrio acting the part of an abandoned man. He puts on a look of pain and suffering that gives him a new sad and mysterious image among our neighbors, especially the women. He has been betrayed by a spoiled Island woman, too proud to come live with him and his poor daughter in this, a basement apartment in the barrio. *¡Pobrecito!* Our family's story, as told by my father, makes him the working-class hero in a fairy tale and Mami the *bruja,* the wicked witch. Yet I knew it was not all an act. I heard him late at night, pacing the floor, and more than once I thought I heard a stifled sob. He missed her just as I did. But a real macho does not admit to crying over a woman. I knew that Papi desperately wanted to complete his transformation into the barrio man. The green Puerto Rican chameleon blending into the browns and grays of our American city. Is this his last evolution? He wants to be verde like the chameleon, but for now, my Papi is blue. And my blue father is singing the old lullaby *"Cielito lindo."*

"Ay, ay, ay, ay," he sings to himself, *"canta y no llores."*

"Sing, and don't cry." That is what the lyrics mean. He used to sing that song to me when I was little. He would hold me and his guitar on his lap and let me play along with him, my little hands wrapped around his strong, hard fingers, callused from his hard job cleaning the tourist beach, and from playing his guitar.

Papi-Azul Sings "Así son las mujeres" (The Way Women Are)

Doña Segura's daughter's leaky sink is a disaster *en progreso*, she yells into our answering machine, for the entire building! If her fifth floor apartment floods, we will all be washed down the street and into the Hudson River! She had left eight messages by the time I got home from school. The last one was a curse in Spanish unless my father showed up by dinnertime.

"*¡Ay, bendito!* These *mujeres* are driving me loco. Es like a *lonplei* album all day long, do this, do that. I tell them they have to *turnearse* for my attention. I only have *dos manos,* even though my *talentos* are multifarious."

My father's Spanglish is impeccable. I love the word *impec-ca-ble*. My mother taught me how to pronounce it after I asked her what she called the kind of English Papi spoke. I remember her laughing: "Your papi speaks impeccable Spanglish."

Growing up I had to choose which of my parents' versions of English I would speak. My mother reminded me often that no tests and no job applications would be written in Spanglish. So I chose her *impeccable* English which I speak with a thick island accent. Now I am learning Spanglish as my third language, my language of adventure, of fun, of survival in the streets of my new home.

"*Hasta la vista,* baby." My father grabs his toolbox and his guitar and looks up at all the stairs he has to climb to reach the place where he will save somebody's day. He shakes his head in dismay.

He is a reluctant hero, my papi-azul.

"*Eres* my superhero, Papi. You are *un supermán.*" He laughs at my awkward attempts at speaking Spanglish. I blow him kisses as he makes his way up the stairs. All the way up I hear my father singing the old song "*Así son (las mujeres)*" with the catchy refrain — that's the way they are (women), that's the way they are when you love them. I hear him tapping the rhythm on the walls of each landing with his toolbox, his guitar slung over his back making a thump-thump sound like the beating of a very big strong heart as he climbs flight after flight.

> *Así son, así son las mujeres*
> *Así son, así son cuando se quieren.*

Seeing Red: Así son los hombres

When I clean our apartment, I have to throw open the door and windows, even if it's winter, to let fresh air clear away the smell of my father's cigars, a new habit he has picked up at the bodega, where the men like to make a tent of smoke around their dominoes game — it must make them feel like boys in a secret clubhouse; it also keeps wives and daughters away. The dominoes room in the bodega is a man's world, a room with only a table and chairs for the players and no place for anyone else to sit. It smells of beer and cigars, odors that are part of the nicotine-yellowed plaster on the walls. Any outsider who enters will emerge smelling like a survivor from a three-alarm fire. Once, when I had not learned the lesson of the dominoes, I went past the safety zone of the bodega to find my father.

Papi had not shown up to eat by seven — I had just heated up a can of red kidney beans and made an *ollita* of white rice for him — so I walked over to Cheo's bodega. I found him in the back at the dominoes table making those mysterious passes over the ivory pieces, which always look to me like a magic trick being performed. He was chewing on the stub of a cigar and nodding to his partner — a secret code. They were playing for money.

"Papi." I stood at the door to the storeroom where they play.

"María, *¿qué haces aquí?* I already ate a sandwich here. Didn't I tell you I'd be late tonight?" I was hurt by his tone, but his eyes told me that he was trying to save face. So I said nothing.

One of the other men, a younger one with freckles and a head of burnt-orange kinky hair, winked at my father.

"She's just doing her duty, hombre. Your daughter is a real mujer now. She wants to take care of her poor abandoned papi."

"Shut up, Iván." My father's tone was a harsh warning so that all talk and movement ceased, and the men turned their eyes away from me.

There was a muffled guffaw from the orange-haired man. Papi continued distributing the dominoes, averting his eyes from them and from me.

"*Está bien,* Papi." I turned on my heel and walked out of the fog of smoke just as the harsh laughter of men erupted. He and I would have to talk later, and I would say I was sorry for having embarrassed him in front of his friends, and he would apologize for doing the same to me. I felt sorry for my father, who was trying as hard as I was to earn a part in the script of our new American life that we have to write for ourselves, every day. *Así somos.* That's the way we are.

Confessions of a Non-Native Speaker

A poem by María Alegre

I confess,
I had to steal English
because what I had
was never enough.
The sly taking
started as a word here,
a word there.
It was easy.
I slipped words
into my pockets,
my crime unnoticed
as the precious *palabras*
spilled out
of unguarded mouths,
and when they were left behind
like empty glasses and china
after a banquet,
or like familiar jewelry,
the everyday gold
tossed anywhere
at bedtime.

I took what I needed
and a little more
from places I slipped easily into
wearing my heavy accent,
my cloak of invisibility.
I slipped in
while the ones who had more
than they could ever use, dreamed
their long, luxurious dreams,
spoiled children
unaware of the real value,
their inherited wealth,
language.

It is different now.
What I had to steal then
is legally mine
since no one has ever claimed
a word, taken back a sentence.
My treasure room is full.
My second language
is a silver cup
from which I intend to drink
the best wine.
Each word I make mine

is a pearl, a diamond,
a ruby, I will someday string
into a necklace
and wear everywhere,
as if I had been born
rich in English.

Judith Ortiz Cofer was born in Puerto Rico and moved to Paterson, New Jersey, as a child. *The New York Times* has deemed her "a writer of authentic gifts, with a genuine and important story to tell." Orchard Books published Cofer's book *An Island Like You: Stories of the Barrio,* which won the Pura Belpré Award and the Américas Award, among many others.

Cofer's other books include *The Meaning of Consuelo,* which was named an ALA Best Book for Young Adults; and *Silent Dancing: A Partial Remembrance of a Puerto Rican Childhood,* which was awarded the 1991 PEN/Martha Albrand Special Citation for Nonfiction and was named a New York Public Library Best Book for the Teen Age. She is the Franklin Professor of English and Creative Writing at the University of Georgia, and lives in Louisville, and Athens, Georgia, with her family.